I0743377

# BEAR'S MISSION

## SEDONA VENEZ

Copyright © 2015 Bear's Mission by Sedona Venez

All rights reserved. This copy is intended for the original purchaser of this book ONLY. No part of this book may be reproduced, scanned, or distributed in any printed or electronic form without prior written permission from the author. Please do not participate in or encourage piracy of copyrighted materials in violation of the authors' rights. Purchase only authorized editions.

Published in the United States of America

This book is a work of fiction. While reference might be made to actual historical events or existing locations, the names, characters, places and incidents are either the product of the authors' imaginations or are used fictitiously, and any resemblance to actual persons, living or dead, business establishments, events, or locales is entirely coincidental.

www.ingramcontent.com/pod-product-compliance
Lightning Source LLC
Chambersburg PA
CBHW070927190726
48292CB00004B/1138

# ABOUT THE AUTHOR

USA TODAY BESTSELLING AUTHOR SEDONA VENEZ lives in New York City with her hot ex-military hubby—hooah— and their fur babies. She loves writing sizzling, sexy intricate stories about strong but broken characters who push limits, overcome their fears and risk it all for love.

*Sedona loves to connect with readers!*
www.sedonavenez.com

# CHAPTER 1

### RAVEN

THE DOOR SLIPPED open and air rushed into the compartment. We were high up in the sky, the land below specks of farms and roads. This always left me breathless, but not in a bad way.

I was definitely doing this by choice.

The adrenaline pumped through my veins as I pictured myself jumping out of the plane. My palms started to sweat. The wind blew across my face as I pulled my goggles down and grinned from ear to ear.

Stepping forward, I shouted through the door in my excitement, "Damn, I love this shit!"

I checked over my parachute pull one last time. Then, with a salute to the men running the show, standing near the doors to assist the rest of the jumpers and me, I leaped out of the airplane and tumbled through the air.

"Yeah!" I yelled in triumph as I went.

Skydiving had always been one of my favorite activities to do with clients who wanted a real nail-biting rush. Shit, I knew it always started my blood pumping. I was an unabashed thrill junkie.

Glancing up, I saw the rest of my party taking off after me into the open sky, one after the other.

Soon, the air was filled with falling rainbow-colored bodies in jumpsuits. They hollered and screamed as they plunged, and I once again realized just how damn lucky I was. This was my highly prized corner office with a sky-blue backdrop all around me. The wind caressed my skin, and I had all the freedom that came from falling through the air with the knowledge that only my parachute would stop me from crashing into the ground.

Everything about my life was perfect—well, almost perfect.

I enjoyed the fall.

When we were at the point when we should pull our chutes, I signaled the rest of the party. Once they all got the message, I pulled my rip cord. My chute opened beautifully, and then I glanced over my shoulder to watch all the others open. We coasted on the wind, guiding ourselves toward the designated landing area.

A few minutes later, I smoothly touched down, running a bit to let my parachute fall behind me. Then I waited for the rest of the party to do the same.

The second we were all on the ground, one of the jumpers pulled off his goggles and waved at me. His tan face glowed from the jump, and he was grinning like a boy on Christmas morning. "Raven, that was by far the best thing I've ever done. I can't believe I've never thought to do this."

I laughed, removing my goggles and hood. "I'm so happy you loved it, Neal. Now, you just need to do this every few months, and you and your board will never be as stressed out over profit margins and new product launches again."

Neal—the tall, lean CEO who'd hired me to lead his group on this little adventure—laughed so hard he doubled over. "I might just take you up on that—as long as you're there to jump with us." His eyes skated over my body with interest. "Now, if I could just get you to agree to have dinner and drinks with me tonight..." He grinned.

Truth be told, I actually got a kick out of being around him, which was new for me. Most of my billionaire clients were cocky

and obnoxious, spending the majority of our outing trying to grope me or bore me with how big their bank accounts were. Neal was quite the opposite. He was just a lovable big guy who liked flirting with me, but there was no way I would break my no-fraternizing-with-clients rule.

His fingers caressed my elbow. "I can regale you with tales about my many adventures in slaying snarling board members consumed with world domination. And you can explain again why such a bright and beautiful woman like you isn't in a relationship."

My lips pressed together as I looked pointedly at his roving fingers. He snatched back his hand.

"As much as I love your company, Neal, I'll have to decline the dinner and drinks invitation," I answered, stepping slightly away from him. "Until our next adventure."

We shook hands as the remainder of the group came over to say their good-byes to me as well. When I finished thanking them, three black SUVs drove up to take them all back to the city.

I steered toward the huge SUV where my assistant, Halle, was waiting, smiling as usual.

Halle jumped out of the driver's side before bouncing over to me. "Damn, that was a pretty wicked dive. I watched most of it from the live feed on your helmet."

"You have to try it," I answered. "How about this weekend?" I wiggled my brows.

Halle shook her head. "Hard pass. You know I don't have the stomach. I'll just stick to being your well-paid minion."

I loved working with Halle, a fresh-out-of-college student who'd always go wide-eyed with every stunt I finished. It made me miss the young exuberance I'd had coming into this business years ago, but at twenty-six, I'd done a lot of living, both good and bad.

"All right. But you don't know what you're missing," I joked while stretching my muscles that had built over the years from

performing stunts. Then I stepped out of my flight suit. All I wanted was a long, hot soak, a glass of wine, and a marathon of mind-numbing reality shows.

I looked over at Halle. "Is that it for the day?"

Halle laughed as she reached into the backseat for a small duffel. "You wish. We're going to dinner to meet with your new clients. They just walked in this morning and were able to get a meeting right away. They must have some deep pockets if they could do that."

It usually took clients a few weeks, even months, before they could meet with one of the other guides or me. A lot of planning went into these trips. Not to mention, background checks would be run on the clients to ensure people like me wouldn't be going on trips with killers or members of a mob. It took preparation and lots of money to get something like this going.

Whatever the clients were paying, it must've been a hell of a lot. I hoped at least the background checks had been completed. I'd prefer not to be stuck with a bunch of psychos on a dangerous adventure where anything could go wrong.

Halle jumped behind the wheel.

"Do you have any idea who they are?" I asked while kicking off my sneakers.

"They work for some finance company—at least, I think they do. I didn't get to hear much before I was told to come get you." Halle's fingers played nervously on the steering wheel. "I saw them when they came in, though, and, Raven, they're a bit odd."

"Lovely. They'd better not be assholes," I groused while tugging my dress pants over my tight yoga bottoms. Then I slipped my suit jacket over the tight black Lycra tank top. My look was complete when I pulled my dark-brown cinnamon hair from my bun and shook it out, allowing it to cascade around my shoulders. Tossing all the discarded items into the bag, I climbed into the SUV.

Halle shook her head. "I wasn't thinking asshole weird, more like creepy or odd. There were seven of them, but only one of

them ever said a word. It was like the others were scared to speak."

I unhappily pursed my lips. "That's strange. Are they new employees?"

Halle shrugged. "No idea. The whole situation was just strange. Though, the guy who did talk was pretty fucking hot." She waggled her eyebrows at me. "A bit rough around the edges, but that beard stubble... Man, I wish I were going with you."

"Interesting," I retorted. "Stilettos in the back?"

"Of course." Halle glanced at me sideways. "It was the first thing I checked."

I just laughed. "I trained you well, grasshopper." I reached into the backseat, taking hold of my sleek stilettos and driving my feet into them. "I only hope you're wrong about these clients. I really don't feel like dealing with a bunch of fucking idiots on a dangerous trip. One horrific experience was enough to last me a damn lifetime."

# CHAPTER 2

## RAVEN

AFTER RUSHING through the door with my eyes darting around, I muttered, "Shit. I'm forty-five minutes late." Looking over at Halle, I inquired, "Do you see them?"

Halle pointed to the guy pacing back and forth. "There's one of them. I believe his name is Josh Price."

My eyes locked on him as we sauntered toward him.

*Goddamn. He's pretty hot.*

He smiled, glancing at Halle and then me. "I was starting to wonder if I got the time wrong."

"That would be my fault, I'm afraid," I explained, stepping forward with my hand out to shake his. "Raven Holiday. I'm the guide the agency has sent for you and your group, Mr. Price. I apologize for my extreme lateness. I jumped out of an airplane not too long ago."

He grinned, holding my hand a bit longer than necessary. "Sounds like you've had quite the day."

A strange jolt shot through my fingers, and I quickly pulled them away.

His smile slipped before his lips tilted up again. "I'm looking forward to our trip together and so is the rest of my group.

We're just right over here," he replied, leading the way to his table.

Halle and I followed him through a maze of tables in the busy restaurant, dodging waiters with trays and businessmen who'd had too much to drink.

"So," Halle whispered before we arrived at the table, "what do you think? Hot but creepy, right?"

I scrunched up my nose. "Hot, but not my type, and something's definitely different about him. But I'm not sure I'd call him creepy." *More like unnerving.*

The last time I'd felt like this, I was surrounded by lions in the great African plains. I'd been out in the wild with clients when we came across a lion pride. In that moment of staring death in the face, I had felt just like this... as if, at any moment, I'd be mauled to death.

I shook my head and tried to concentrate on the meeting at hand. "We'll talk about this later," I whispered to Halle.

When we eventually stopped, I took a long look at all of them and wondered why the hair along the rear of my neck was suddenly standing on end. The impression from earlier intensified tenfold, and I tried not to wince. Glancing around, I looked for an air vent but didn't see one.

After the introductions to four men and two women, Halle and I sat down at the table and started in on the details of the trip.

"So," I began with a forced smile, "I hear from Halle that you're looking to go on an adventure in Canada?" I arched a brow. "A four-week camping trip, starting the first week of December? Quite an outing to take for beginners like yourselves."

They all nodded, but Josh spoke. "Yes, we thought a get-together would help us bond. Some of us are new to the company. What better way to get to know your new colleagues than a camping trip out in the wild? This has been a big year for

us, and I thought it was time to celebrate our achievements in a unique way."

I scowled at his lighthearted speech. They all seemed excited, but none of them looked like they were used to surviving in the outdoors. The deep woods of Canada was a rugged place with no room for overzealous white-collared executives. Things could always take a quick turn for the worse, especially coming into this season. Snowfall wasn't uncommon this time of year, and that brought a chance for storms and dangerously low temperatures.

"This isn't just some ordinary camping trip you want me to plan, and I need to make sure you all understand this," I emphasized, laying my hands flat on the table. "The wilderness up north is dangerous. If you're not careful, if you don't play by the rules and follow my lead, you could end up hurt or dead." I stared them down.

Except for Halle, every single person at the table seemed to twitch at my words, but none of them appeared worried.

*Who are these fucking people?*

From what Halle had explained, they had no experience with a trip like this, yet none showed the slightest bit of apprehension. I waited to see if anyone would respond to my words.

Once again, only Josh answered me. "We understand. Now, let's go over our itinerary, shall we? We have a lot to plan and little time to get it all ready to go."

I nodded, a bit unsettled at their reactions, as I tried to silence the warning bells jingling in my head. Every fiber of my body was screaming that this trip was a clusterfuck waiting to happen.

Beckoning the waiter over, I said, "Please bring your wine menu." I was going to need all the liquid courage I could get to soothe my suddenly frayed nerves. I just hoped my gut instincts were wrong.

～

*THE SKY WAS DARK AS PELTS OF ICY SNOW BEAT AGAINST MY BODY. My teeth chattered loudly. My clothes were drenched as I pushed through the dense forest.*

*Despair and confusion clouded my mind.*

*Where am I?*

*With my body dragging, I felt like I had been walking forever with no destination. My feet sloshed through the snow mixed with mud. The farther I plowed into the wilderness, the more concerned I became.*

*Keep going, Raven, I repeated over and over in my head.*

*Pushing one snow-ladened branch out of the path, I trod into a big clearing. I took one step and heard the ice cracking beneath my foot, plunging me into the frigid water.*

*"Help," I croaked into the darkness.*

*I clawed at the edge of the hole, but to no avail. It crumbled under my fingers as I sloshed about. I was becoming hypothermic as tears slid down my cheeks.*

*I was going to die—alone.*

*"Please," I whimpered.*

*The trees around the clearing rustled, and a gigantic bear bounded through it. It roared while racing toward me. On its back were streaks of golden fur. Its teeth were terrifyingly huge, but his eyes... They were sky blue.*

*I shook my head in confusion. This couldn't be right. Bears didn't have blue eyes.*

*The bear sidled up to me, tilting its head in inquiry. I almost swallowed my tongue when it reared up on its hind legs and growled. I shouted out in terror.*

I SAT STRAIGHT UP IN BED, GASPING, AS I'D DONE SEVERAL nights before. The dreams had become more intense, and each time, the same bear would appear.

I swung my legs over the edge of the mattress and leaned forward with my elbows on my knees and my face in my hands.

My heart was racing as I tried to shake off the overwhelming uneasiness, thinking these dreams were a bad omen of things to come.

Something was terribly wrong, and I didn't know what it was. I had a bad feeling it was linked to my upcoming trip with Josh Price and his team.

My final meeting with them had been one of the oddest interactions I'd ever experienced with any client. After we had gone through the itinerary, he'd wanted to get to know me a bit. He'd asked about my family and my friends and if my absence from home during the holiday season would be an issue. Most clients wouldn't ask about my personal life, and I really didn't like it when people pried. I'd managed not to tell him anything about myself, because, frankly, my life wasn't that interesting.

My story was like most other orphans'. I hadn't seen the point of explaining where I'd come from when, honestly, I didn't care. The fact that I had been abandoned as a baby and brought up in a series of foster homes had made me stronger and a bit of a loner, but it didn't define me.

I hoped I'd last the whole four weeks and I wouldn't come back with bruised and broken clients for my bosses to deal with. They'd gone twenty years without a lawsuit. I was pretty sure they'd fire my ass if I were the one to break that streak.

The best-case scenario would be if Josh and his team tapped out before the four weeks were over. They wouldn't be the first clients to do so, and that was why my bosses had a no-refund policy.

Hence, I had a contingency plan. If Josh and his team couldn't make it through the whole four weeks, they would have to handle their own transportation out of the wild.

# CHAPTER 3

## RAVEN

Day one of the trip, I tried to relax as the helicopter dropped us off at our starting point. In four weeks, we would circle back to this point to be picked up. I'd planned everything accordingly, so as long as we stuck to our schedule, we'd be on time.

Halle handed my pack to me and glanced around at the rest of the group. "I wish I could stay with you. Some of these guys are hot. Damn, even the two women are pretty attractive," Halle whispered. "And they're all freaking rich. That's always a big plus. I took a glance at the check Mr. Price wrote. Holy shit, Raven. If you were looking for a sexy billionaire, I'd say he's your man," she said quietly.

"I'm not interested," I proclaimed, trying to keep it light. But the hair on the back of my neck was up again. I was used to that sensation when I was getting ready to leap out of an airplane or go bungee jumping, but never when I was just standing around people.

I'd noticed my apprehension elevated mostly around Josh.

Over the last couple of meetings, I'd gotten the same weird reaction when I was around him, but all the background checks had come back clean. He was the new CEO of a Manhattan-based company that was doing extremely well. And as my bosses

had reminded me, he was bound to do business with them again if he was satisfied with this trip. They'd drilled it into my head that I should ensure Mr. Price had a wonderful time so he'd come back and tell the rest of his board members and friends about it. They'd do anything to draw in more rich clients. If I wasn't being paid as much as I was for this trip, I would've swallowed my fake smile and told my bosses to fuck off.

"Yeah, well," Halle responded with a shrug, "have fun without me. Everything is in your bag. You have the satellite phone, and the walkie-talkies are already set to the local channels of the Canadian Rangers. I think I also packed enough first aid kits to save you from a bear attack."

I glowered. "Really? If one of us is attacked by a bear, I don't think bandages will help."

She snickered quietly. "You never know. All right, it looks like your group is ready to go." She gave me a quick hug and then waved good-bye to everyone else. "I'll see you all in four weeks."

We watched Halle get back into the helicopter, and then it took off.

I turned around to address the group and flinched when I saw Josh intently watching me, almost hungrily. For a second, I was worried and thought about calling Halle back, but then he smiled and came to stand beside me. It was a weird switch, and I tried not to let it bother me. I wasn't exactly a greedy person, but my bosses had been paying me well for five years. I could handle a few strange people for four weeks.

"Raven, we'll follow your lead," Josh announced.

I nodded and cleared my throat, hoping the sudden nervousness would disappear once we were underway. "Everyone has their packs on tight? We've got a few miles to go today before we get to our first campsite."

"I think we'll be all right," Josh stated.

"We'll keep up. If not, just leave the newbie for the bears," Boyle, one of the other associates, drawled with a wink as he gave a friendly shove to who I thought was Owen.

Boyle was large, taller and burlier than Josh. A scar ran up the side of his right cheek and disappeared into his ebony hairline. I'd noticed it yesterday, but today, for some reason, it stood out from his harshly lined face.

"Owen's got enough meat on his bones to slow down a bear."

I sighed and reminded myself to maintain my cool. They were new to this. I would have to give them a few days to understand what they had gotten themselves into.

I eyed the entire team—Price, Boyle, Ian, Owen, Brian, Maggie, and Brenda. "If a bear attacks us, we won't be leaving anyone behind," I scolded. "You'll do exactly as I say and nothing more if you want to live."

"Oh, come on, Raven, we're just having a little fun," Josh told me.

"There will be plenty of fun, but I need to know all of you will also take your safety seriously. This is not a joke. We're not in some movie. This is reality, and if one of us gets seriously injured, it could require hours or days for help to reach us, if they can reach us at all," I stated.

Josh turned to his companions and raised his eyebrows. "Agreed. Right, everyone? Raven's in charge. We do exactly as she says."

For a second, I thought I saw every one of them bow their heads to Josh before he turned back to me and nodded. I read that as the signal they were ready to set out. I pulled out my compass to ensure we would be heading northeast, toward our objective.

Josh and his team talked as we hiked through the wild. I listened but concentrated on just getting to the campsite. Their conversation really wasn't making much sense to me anyway. They continued speaking about business back home and getting things completed in time before the big day. I didn't want to eavesdrop. I needed to keep my ears tuned in to other noises around us.

*Just get through day one*, I repeated over and over as I trekked up a steep hill.

I didn't want anything to happen, but I wanted to make sure they all knew what they were getting into for the next four weeks. Besides, it wasn't as if they would really be roughing it. The only thing they had to do when they reached the campsite was set up the tents. A stash of supplies was at each place we would be camping at over the next four weeks, thanks to the money Josh had supplied to the company I worked for.

It had taken almost two months just to get everything set up. Josh had been specific about every part of this trip, not that I minded. Each phase had been planned out well.

A few hours into the hike, I started to get a bit tired, and I was ready to call for a short break, but none of them were. Not one of them was out of breath, looked exhausted, or even red in the face. I was in good shape, but my thighs, particularly my quads, burned from the exertion.

"Anyone need a break?" I called out anyway. "Ready to grab some water and a quick snack before we head onward?"

"Sure," Josh agreed. "Break, everyone."

They all removed their packs and found seats on the ground as I removed mine and pulled out a granola bar. I walked a few yards away and checked our surroundings. So far, everything was fine. The temperature was chilly, but not overly frigid. I had checked the weather reports for this week, and no storms had been on the radar. The Rangers had promised they'd get ahold of me somehow if something big was headed our way.

Thank goodness the trip was going well so far, but that was what worried me. I wasn't sure why, but I wasn't as comfortable as I normally would be out in the wilderness, away from the city.

"So how are we doing so far?" Josh asked.

I turned, finishing a gulp of water, and forced a grin onto my face. "Well, no one's passed out yet or fallen into a hole, so all in all, I'd say everyone's doing pretty well for amateurs." I played

with my water bottle for a second before glancing up at him. "Are you sure none of you guys have hiking experience?"

"Not that they've told me about. They're just really excited to be out here."

I nodded, but I wasn't convinced. "I think it's time to get moving again. You want to tell everyone to pack up? We won't break again until we arrive at the first encampment. Maybe we'll do some fishing for dinner tonight."

"Sounds good. I'll tell the others." Josh headed to his group and told them to pack up and move out.

A few minutes later, they were back on the trail, following me through the wild.

# CHAPTER 4

## BEAR

MY BREATH CREATED tiny white puffs from the cold air. I crouched down under the tree cover and stared at the multiple sets of footprints. A large party with five or maybe six individuals had passed through the spot not too long ago.

I took a deep breath and smelled the dense forest air. Something wasn't right about the stench, but until I had a visual, I had nothing to go on except these tracks, and they told me little about who was in this traveling party.

"Beta to Alpha, have you found a visual?" Cutter's voice came over my radio.

I pressed my earpiece tighter against my ear as I clicked the button on the radio at my shoulder. "Alpha to Beta, that's a negative. Footprints heading north. Multiples, but no visual. I repeat, no visual."

"Orders?"

"Meet me at the first rendezvous point. Alpha out." I clicked off the radio and straightened.

I tightly gripped the rifle in my hands before slinging it over my shoulder. With two shoulder holsters, which carried at least three knives among other things, I was prepared for anything

that might cross my path. However, a wild animal wasn't what I wanted to find today.

People had made these tracks.

I scanned the trees, but there were no other tracks besides the footprints. Growling deep in annoyance, I trudged toward the rendezvous point to meet up with the rest of my team. Perhaps they had more information to help me understand why this mission was quickly turning from simple to dangerous. But we had our orders, and I never missed my mark—ever.

A few minutes of heavy hiking and I was at the river. From what I could tell, the group had passed this way, out of the neutral territory. The rest of my team, Cutter and Grant, stood alert, waiting for me.

My second-in-command, Cutter, stepped forward and nodded toward the north. He casually flung a knife up and down as he uttered, "From what we can tell, they're setting up camp about three miles that way."

"You had a visual?" I demanded.

"No, but a campsite is there and ready to go. We waited for most of the day, but there's been no sign of them so far," Cutter explained. "What do you think, Bear?"

I rubbed my jaw and gazed across the river. "We'll stake out the camp but keep our distance. I want to be certain of how many people we're dealing with."

"Understood," Cutter agreed.

"Let's get moving, Grant," I ordered.

Grant, the third and final member of my team, didn't answer. He gazed toward the tree line with a dark look, his tan fingers raking across his stark white hair. His solemn silence was normal, but out of the three of us, he was by far more dangerous to cross, which was why I'd recruited him for my team. Grant was loyal to a fault, and he never backed down.

I trudged onward, leading Cutter and Grant toward a ridge overlooking the campsite. By nightfall, I hoped we'd have a visual of our target.

# CHAPTER 5

## RAVEN

BY THE TIME the group and I reached the campsite, the sun was starting to go down, but there was still enough light to fish. So once we dumped our gear and got a fire going, I led them down to the riverbank. When I turned to instruct them on the proper way to fish, I saw they were already casting lines and teasing each other about who would catch the bigger fish for dinner.

I glowered but kept my mouth closed.

I decided when we reached the next site, I was going to call Halle to find out if she could dig up other information on them. They obviously had more experience than they had acknowledged.

I eased myself down onto a slab of rock I'd picked as my fishing spot, when I got a weird feeling in the nether part of my belly. Peeking about, I winced when I found Josh staring at me so intensely the hair on the nape of my neck stood on end, as usual. For a second, I felt the pressing need to move away, but then it died as he worked his way over to me.

"Mind if I join you?" he asked.

"Help yourself," I replied as he plopped down next to me. "If we don't catch anything, there's food locked in a metal crate in one of the tents."

"I'm certain they'll hook something at some point. So tell me more about yourself, besides the fact that you like to jump out of airplanes and take random people on trips into the wilderness," he added with a wink.

I rammed my fishing pole into the dirt beside the rock. "There's not much else to say."

"Oh, there has to be something. Does your love of adventure come from your parents?"

An old anger started to raise its head, but I promptly stomped it down. *Relax, Raven. He's just curious, not prying.*

There was no reason for me to bite his head off, but if he kept pushing, I was going to go straight New York crazy on his ass.

"I was abandoned as a kid, and I grew up in foster homes."

"Sad to hear that."

I shrugged and smiled. "It's all right. I turned out fine."

"So you don't know who your parents are?"

"Nope, never tried to find them either," I snarled. "Figured if they didn't want me, then I didn't want them."

"I can understand that. So where does your adventurous spirit come from?"

I turned to him. "I don't know and don't care. Look, I'm trying to be polite, but don't you think this whole conversation is a bit too personal?"

Immediately, he held up his hands. "Sorry. I didn't realize it was a touchy subject."

"It's not a sensitive topic, but you going all investigative reporter on me is grating on my nerves." I took a deep breath and let it out, straining to get a grip on my mood. "I apologize. I'm just not really good with conversations. Usually, I don't have a chance to actually speak with the people I go on trips with."

He just laughed. "Too busy falling out of airplanes?"

"Something like that." I hesitated. "What about you? I know your company is headquartered in Manhattan. Are you a native New Yorker?"

"No. I move around a lot."

"Hmm... Lots of traveling?"

"No. Lots of running away from the law."

I stiffened instantly.

He just snickered. "It's not what you think. I left home when I was young. Bounced around for a bit and got into heaps of trouble." He nodded over in Boyle's direction. "I met Boyle along the way. We were both headstrong and loners, so it wasn't an easy friendship, but we had a great deal in common. Years later, here we are, two misfit millionaires sitting in the center of nowhere, camping."

I sat in silence, sorting through Josh's story. A lot of it rang true, but the slivers of information he'd left out were troubling. I watched two others catch a fish each, big ones, and I shook my head.

*They've never been fishing before, my ass.*

I exhaled sharply. Maybe I was reading too much into Josh's and his team's behavior. Frankly, it wasn't any of my business. As long as they had a good time and no one got hurt or killed, I'd get paid a hefty bonus at the end of the trip.

After a few more fish were caught, we headed back to the campsite and made dinner. Sitting in the firelight, I couldn't help the laughter that slipped out at their antics and joking. They seemed more like family than coworkers, only they looked nothing alike. I glanced across the campground and grimaced when my eyes swiftly locked with Josh's intense stare.

*Shit.*

He was getting creepy again. If he kept watching me like a hawk, I was going to say something, and it wouldn't be nice.

The sun had gone down, and we were surrounded by darkness as the bugs came out to play. I shooed away a flying insect and caught Josh's eyes once more. He nodded to me, and I tried to smile back, but my lips wouldn't move.

His freaky eyes had a strange amber glow. I peered around the campsite and nearly choked. All of their eyes were glowing. I

was fascinated by their sheer beauty. Suddenly, my mind became cloudy, my vision fuzzy, and then my brain went blank.

I blinked at him in confusion.

*Where the hell am I?*

My hands trembled as I had thoughts so jumbled that the harder I tried to unravel them, the more difficult it became to clear my head.

Taking a cleansing deep breath, I concentrated on settling my mind, and the confusion started to ebb away.

*What the fuck was that?*

Never in my life had I experienced something so disorientating and scary. I stood up on wobbly legs. "Guys, it's been a long day. I'm turning in early. Make sure to allow the fire to burn down to embers."

I didn't even wait for a response before turning on my heel and hightailing it away.

# CHAPTER 6

## BEAR

*WHAT THE FUCK?* I whiffed the air once more to be certain. *A human female?* I stared down at the camp.

We were high up on a ridge overlooking the group. Cutter and Grant were spread out a bit farther away. We needed an exact number, and for damn sure, we didn't need a human in the middle of this shit.

I shook my head in disbelief. *Did she even know what she was doing? No, more importantly, did she recognize who the hell these people actually were?*

"Beta to Alpha," Cutter drawled.

"Alpha. Go," I snarled, growing angrier by the damn second.

"Do my eyes deceive me, or is that an unknown with our group?"

"It is." I stayed where I was, lying flat on the ground, watching the woman get up and disappear into her tent.

Then I eyed the main target, calmly sitting there on a log, hungrily watching the woman's tent. The female was of no concern to me. I was only focused on my target.

*Damn. Should we move in while she's out of the way?*

*No.*

The noise would draw her out, and I wasn't about to have

innocent blood on my hands. If she got in the way when we made our move, there would be no guarantee she wouldn't get taken out with the rest of them.

I growled. "We can't move in until we know who she is. Tell Grant to take some pics, and then we'll set up camp for the night."

"Got it."

# CHAPTER 7

### RAVEN

A FEW MORE DAYS HAD GONE BY, and Josh had started opening up a bit more about his life. Surprisingly, he and I had a lot more in common than I'd originally thought. We were both castaways who had grown up with no family.

I had to admit, I wasn't used to being around people for long periods of time—or at least people who actually talked to me. Josh and his team had been making an honest effort to get to know who I was instead of just treating me as their guide.

As we continued on our trek through the wilderness, Josh had been walking with me each day. In fact, he'd been bonding more with me than with the rest of the group. And he was starting to seem less like another rich asshole who was trying to hit on me.

We stopped by a stream for a break as week one was slowly coming to a close.

Strangely, I found myself drawn to Josh.

His muscles tensed as he crouched down to refill his water bottle, and I felt my chest tighten. Something about him was both intriguing and frightening.

"I can feel you staring at me from over here," he joked without turning my way.

I cleared my throat, mentally kicking myself. "Sorry. I was just thinking about something."

"Oh yeah? And what's that?" He stood and headed toward me. He took a swig of water, and it ran down his stubbled chin.

I watched him until I realized I was doing it again, and I shook my head. "Nothing. Just wondering if your group would like to try their hand at hunting some small game for dinner?"

"I'm sure they wouldn't mind a few pointers from you." He wiped the water from his chin with his sleeve and winked.

"I doubt they'll need any such help from me."

He shrugged his muscular shoulders. "Never know. We've never met anyone like you before." He reached his hand up and gently pushed the hair that had fallen from my bun back behind my ear. "Your skin is even more beautiful in this light."

"Thanks," I croaked.

*What the hell is wrong with me?*

I took a step back. "Let's get moving!" I yelled to the team. "We'll hunt for game as we head to the next site. We'll be at that one for a few nights," I announced. Then I turned and continued forward, knowing they'd catch up quickly enough.

WE'D JUST FINISHED A DINNER THAT INCLUDED RABBITS AND even a few geese. I hadn't been surprised by their hunting skills. I was just confused as to why they had all tried to act so lost when they seemed to know more than I did about surviving in the outdoors.

Boyle and Owen were the ones who had brought in the rabbits. When I'd asked how they'd caught them, Boyle just winked, and Owen smirked. The two women in the group, Maggie and Brenda, had returned with the geese, but as far as I knew, none of them had a weapon, besides knives.

*So how the hell did they manage to kill them?*

Josh, Ian, and Brian had gone with me. I'd shown them how

to make traps to catch rabbits and then how to kill them quickly and efficiently once they had been caught. I'd thought I heard them snicker behind me, but when I'd turned around, they had been solemnly and intently watching me.

As the evening got darker, I wandered away from camp, observing the stars from beneath the trees. They were so beautiful, clear, and crisp. There was no light pollution to dim them. If I could live out here forever, I would, but every now and again, I wanted to hear some city noise.

I'd been alone all my life. I wasn't about to spend the rest of my existence wandering around the wilderness with no one around at all. I could do it for a while maybe, but not forever.

Away from the fire, I was cold, so I wrapped my arms around my body. I didn't want to go back to the campsite yet. I needed a few moments to get a grip on my thoughts before they started to spiral too far out of control.

Josh and his team weren't mean or threatening. They were just strange. I'd dealt with plenty of strange people before. Hell, I was one, too. Not many people would consider what I did on a daily basis as normal.

A smile lit my lips as I thought about the past few years of working for the agency and all the places I'd gone, like exotic places that very few people had ever heard of.

The life I led was incredible.

I noticed a few clouds rolling in from the west, and I took a deep breath and then exhaled, letting go of all the stress that had built up since this trip started.

*Everything is going to be fine. It always is.*

There was only one time when things hadn't gone according to plan, and I would think about it every time before I set out on a trip.

"You seem to be deep in thought," Josh remarked right behind me.

I jumped, startled. "Shit."

"Sorry, I didn't mean to sneak up on you."

"You're just so damn quiet." Leaning against a tree, I turned my gaze back upward. "I was just thinking about life. I tend to do that a lot when I'm out here."

"Understandable. It's so quiet with no one around to bother you."

I nodded in agreement and then glanced at him. "Well, except for you."

"Ouch." He smirked. "Now, that one hurt. I can go away if you'd like?"

"No, you can stay."

He walked over to me and looked up at the stars. "So what were you thinking about so intently?"

"The reason I'm always telling you and your team to be careful," I shared.

"What happened?"

I breathed out heavily and hung my head as I remembered that trip to the mountains. We had been in the Rockies, and everything had happened so quickly. It was a miracle no one died.

"I was in charge of a large group like this. We were hiking high up in the Rockies. A storm came out of nowhere, and there was a rockslide. One of the younger members of my group got pinned. I stayed with him through the entire thing, holding his hand. Despite all of my hoping and praying, I knew I was going to lose him, but then help finally arrived." I shuddered, remembering when they'd pulled him free. His legs had been so mangled that I'd recognized he'd never walk again.

Josh reached out, placing a hand on my shoulder. "I'm sorry, Raven, but you don't have to worry so much about us. We'll manage."

I just laughed. "Yeah, I'm kind of realizing that."

I laid my hand over his. His fingers closed around mine as he stepped nearer.

A voice inside my head warned me to take a deep breath and

push him away, but my heart was pounding away with excitement. I froze like a deer caught in headlights.

He stepped closer until we were inches from each other. He was a full head taller than me as he stared down into my upturned face. His gaze locked on mine.

"Raven." He breathed my name like a prayer.

Lost in a sudden wave of arousal, I rose onto my toes and pressed my lips against his soft, warm lips. The kiss deepened quickly, and I imagined I heard him grumble as he enfolded his arms around me.

I was on fire with a need I'd never felt before. It threw me, but I didn't stop to analyze it.

Josh's hand inched down to grip my hip as he ground his lower half against mine. I felt his bulge against my stomach as I deepened our kiss.

*This was insane.*

The searing heat running through my body and the unexplainable impulse to be one with this man was utterly consuming.

When he began to kiss his way down my neck, I experienced a brief bit of lucidity.

"Stop," I hissed.

"What's wrong?"

"I can't do this," I murmured. "You're a client."

"So?" His hold tightened.

"So let me the fuck go," I demanded.

He nodded before letting go of me and backing away. My knees almost buckled when another wave of need rushed through my body. Dismissing it, I hurried away.

# CHAPTER 8

## BEAR

From a distance, we watched Price and the human kissing. I clenched my fists hard, and Cutter whistled.

"Damn, Bear. She looks like a fucking good kisser. If she survives this, I might have to test her out myself."

I smacked Cutter upside the head. "Stop eye-fucking her, you pervert. We're here to watch Price and his group, not the woman making out with him."

I didn't mention that the second I'd seen them kissing, something black, vile, and vicious reared up inside my head.

*Jealousy.*

My gut ached as if someone had been repeatedly kicking it.

*What the fuck?*

This woman meant nothing to me, yet I felt the urge to break cover and rush over to them to smash in Price's fucking teeth.

Grant smirked.

Cutter rubbed the back of his head. "Fine, she's off-limits. So when are we making our move?"

"We have visual confirmation, but you know the rules," I responded.

"Your rules or their rules?" Cutter asked with a lifted eyebrow.

"Mine, you moron. I won't go in until we know for sure she's a member of his pack."

Josh's pack was notoriously traditional and didn't breed with humans like other wolf-shifter packs did.

*So what was this human doing with them?*

But I had another reason for my rule of waiting before charging in, claws first. The one time we'd rushed in, after getting a visual of our target, the people had been innocent of the crimes I'd been told they had committed. I'd known we should have waited to watch them actually shift to know for sure if they were what my squad and I hunted.

Never again would I make the same damn error.

Grant nudged me and pointed. "I guess they're done with their foreplay for the night."

I looked on as Price headed back to the fire and the woman vanished into her tent. "Good. Cutter, you have first watch. Wake me up in two hours."

"Yeah, yeah. Whatever you say," Cutter responded dryly.

I growled in warning, sensing Cutter's unexpected need for a fight, but I wasn't in the fucking mood. I needed to get my suddenly frayed thoughts together.

Walking to find a comfortable place in the soil, I sat down beneath a tree and closed my eyes, hoping to have a dreamless sleep, but all I caught was that damn woman's beautiful face.

# CHAPTER 9

### RAVEN

I CALLED the local ranger station, which unfortunately was nowhere near us, and checked in to let them know of my group's progress. We talked for a few minutes to verify my group was still well supplied and the weather would hold out. I was told the temperature should stay steady, but they'd let me know if it was going to drop drastically. I thanked the ranger and then hung up.

I had the phone for a long time in my hand before finally deciding I needed to tell somebody about what had happened with Josh.

I dialed Halle's number, knowing I'd likely be yelled at for using the satellite phone for personal reasons, and I waited impatiently for her to pick up.

After five rings, I finally heard her voice come on the line. "Hello?"

"Halle, it's Raven."

"Hey. Why are you calling? Is something wrong?" She yawned loudly. "You know you're going to get your ass chewed out for using this phone, right?"

"Don't care about that shit right now," I murmured.

"So something is wrong?" Halle asked.

"No, not exactly. Shit, maybe. I don't know," I answered,

holding my head. "Damn, I think I might have crossed a line. Now I'm not exactly sure what to do about it." *There.* It was now out in the open.

Silence radiated from the other end before she asked, "Wait, did you sleep with Josh?"

"What? Fuck no—not yet at least." *Shit, I sounded like some skanky whore.*

Halle laughed. "Oh man, Raven, breaking your own rules?"

I blew out with frustration. "It's not funny," I argued. "We just kind of made out against a tree a few minutes ago. I'm not even sure why I did it." I really wasn't. Yes, Josh was hot, but he really wasn't my type.

"You find him attractive. I don't blame you. He's gorgeous, Raven."

I wanted to disagree. Something was still bugging me about him. "Can you do me a favor when you get in tomorrow?"

"Sure. What do you need?"

"See what you can dig up on Josh Price. Something about him doesn't seem right."

"Raven, he passed the background checks. I'm sure he's fine. You're probably just nervous... When was the last time you had sex?"

"Months," I blurted out.

"Exactly. That's the problem. You need some stress relief."

I wanted to quibble with Halle, but I really couldn't. It had been much too long since I allowed a man into my body, but I was pretty sure I didn't want to fuck Josh.

"Please just do this for me, Halle."

Another long pause told me she was trying to figure out what was really going on with me.

"Are you in trouble?" she asked. "Because if you are, I'll have someone fly in and get you out ASAP."

"No, I'm fine. Just check him out for me. Maybe the agency's background investigation missed something. Do some digging

into his social life, and as soon as you get anything, call me or let the rangers know."

"Will do. I'll see what I can find."

There was silence, and then she asked, "Raven, are you sure you're all right?"

"Yeah," I chirped, trying to sound as if nothing was wrong. All the while, I felt like I was losing my fucking mind. "I'm good. Talk to you soon."

I hung up and lay back on my sleeping bag, trying to relax. My mind kept wandering back to how I'd felt while Josh was kissing me. I'd never felt like that before with any man—out of control and desperate to have him in any sexual position he wanted. But it wasn't natural. *Is something compelling me to give Josh what he wants—me?*

Besides, Josh was too polished and perfect. Normally, I steered clear of those types of men for good reason. None of them wanted forever. And I was done with one-night stands. However, I was smart enough to know there was no such thing as a white knight who would come in to save me from my loneliness.

After a few minutes, I rolled onto my stomach and buried my head under my pillow.

Sleep—that was what I needed to set my mind right.

We would be staying at the campsite for a few nights, and we didn't have much to do except explore the area around us and enjoy the wilderness. Maybe we'd do some swimming in some hot springs. It'd be ungodly cold, but that was exactly what I needed to get my libido under control. A nice icy dip could clear my head and get my heated body back to normal.

# CHAPTER 10

## BEAR

I paced back and forth, scanning the campsite. My right eye twitched as it would when I felt my emotions raging out of control.

*I don't need this shit.*

I couldn't shake the need to charge down into that camp and rip out Price's windpipe. And it wasn't because Price was the target. It was the thought of how he'd been so close to that woman, touching her and kissing her.

My inner bear roared.

The muscles in my shoulders bunched. I'd never felt a primal urge like this before, and it was threatening to tear me apart from the inside out if I didn't do something about it.

*Fuck.*

The growling in my head started, and I snarled aloud, trying to drown it out. It didn't calm my inner bear. It only pissed him off, making him press against my skin.

He wanted out—to fight, to mate, to claim the human.

*Shit, I don't have time for this.*

I needed to focus on catching Price and returning him to the facility to pay for his crimes and to help lead us to bigger fish. That was the main goal of this mission, and I wasn't about to

fuck it up because of some woman who had gotten herself caught in the middle of this clusterfuck. She would figure out soon enough who she was dealing with—or kissing under the moonlight. It was no concern of mine.

My bear rumbled with displeasure.

The fire at their campsite started to die down, and I watched from a distance as, one by one, the others in Price's group turned in for the night, except for one. A sole figure made his way to the woman's tent.

My body tensed, ready to strike.

*Boyle.*

*What is he going to do? Is he going to attack?*

He didn't try to go into her tent, but he stayed outside, crouched low, as if listening to something. I sniffed the air and cursed when I smelled the spike of tension exuding from Boyle, wafting into the air.

Something was wrong.

It took a great deal of effort for me not to lose control right then, but I managed to keep myself calm, breathing deeply, as I observed Boyle make his way back through the camp, disappearing into another tent.

For whatever reason, Price had brought his group to the wild. I had a feeling I was running out of time to stop whatever he was planning from happening. We'd have to move in closer, and I hoped to bring Josh and his pack down before it was too late.

# CHAPTER 11

## RAVEN

I woke up early, as I always did, ready to get breakfast going, only to find the fire was already roaring and Price was up along with the rest of the camp. He'd started making breakfast, and his group was sitting around drinking coffee and chatting excitedly with each other. I wondered what had gotten them all in such a chipper mood as I stretched, stifling a yawn.

"Morning," I greeted, heading over. "What time is it?"

Price winked at me. "Oh, you didn't oversleep. Don't worry. We all just thought we'd make you breakfast since you've kept us alive this far. Week one is complete, and not a hair is out of place."

"That's nice of you," I replied, sitting down in my camp chair.

The warmth of the fire reached my toes and fingertips as I held them out. It felt nice. I'd been toasty in my tent all night, burrowed deep in my low-temperature sleeping bag and wearing all the essential undergarments for this type of weather. But having a fire was always so much better.

For a few minutes, I just let the fire heat my skin as I inhaled the woodsy scent. Alarm bells started going off in my head, and I

opened my eyes to see Josh watching me as intently as he continually did.

"Really," I insisted, clearing my throat at the awkward feeling, "thanks for cooking."

"We don't mind. Besides, today is a big day."

I mentally ran through our itinerary, but nothing came to mind. "And why is that?"

Boyle stalked over with an armful of firewood and leered at me, making me extremely uncomfortable. "It's the anniversary of our company. We've been around for a long time."

"And we plan on being around for a hell of a lot longer," Maggie added loudly.

They all cheered with her, and I felt as if I were missing something.

"That's great," I chimed in, hoping my voice was cheerful enough to cover my suspicions. "Maybe we'll just relax today and play a few games."

"I think we're up for that," Josh exclaimed. "A few rounds of Capture the Flag?"

"I don't see why not," I responded. "As long as everyone stays fairly close to camp, we should be fine. Haven't seen any bears this whole trip, so we should be safe enough. But that doesn't mean I want anyone to let their guard down. Don't need someone falling off a ridge or into the river."

Everyone nodded in agreement and swore they'd keep an eye out for danger. Josh smirked and met eyes with Boyle. The latter winked before heading off to gather more wood, while Josh took a long, hard look into the trees around us.

After breakfast, we divided into two teams. Boyle and Josh both gave one of their shirts to be flags, and for the next few hours, I ran around the woods with this interesting group of people.

After we started playing, my thoughts kept going back to the satellite phone in my tent, wondering if Halle had found

anything out yet. Something just wasn't sitting well with me about Josh and his group.

Throughout the game, those thoughts kept getting worse. I was on a different team than Josh, and every time I thought I was about ready to sneak around and grab their flag, he'd appear right behind me.

It was eerie how he constantly seemed to know where I was.

One time, I swore I heard him sniffing loudly right behind me, and he wasn't the only one. Even if I couldn't see any of the others, somehow, they unfailingly found me, sniffing the air, as if it wasn't strange to be doing it so noisily. The way they seemed to smell me and follow my trail through the maze of trees was unnerving. No matter how quietly I moved, one would appear around a tree trunk and capture me. I tried to act like it didn't bother me, but they would have a strange predatory look in their eyes every time.

I attempted to brush it off, but when the game ended, the first thing I did was head to my tent to check the satellite phone.

But when I looked through my bag for it, the phone was gone.

"What the hell?"

I dug through everything, and then I got down on my hands and knees and checked every inch of my tent. It was definitely gone, and so were the other radios I had in case of emergency. Someone had been in my tent.

Heat pumped through my body as my fists balled tightly.

*What the fuck?*

*Who's gone through my stuff?*

*Dammit.*

*What the hell will happen if one of them gets hurt?* Help wouldn't be here for hours, maybe even days.

This wasn't a fucking game, and I was tired of them acting like it was.

Pissed, I rushed out of the tent. "Josh!" I yelled.

"What?" he asked, hurrying over to me.

"Someone stole our radios and the satellite phone. Those were our only means of communication in case something happened to one of us," I snapped. "Someone went through my tent to get them."

"Team, get here right now!" he yelled.

Everyone gathered around.

"Who stole the radios?"

Everyone turned to stare at their neighbors and shrugged. No one was willing to fess up, and I wasn't about to stay out in the wilderness with no radio. I might be a thrill-seeker, but I wasn't stupid. No radio meant there wasn't a way to call for help. If anything did go wrong, we were totally alone, miles from anyone who could help.

"This isn't a damn game," I snapped. "Whoever took them needs to hand them over right now. Otherwise, we're turning around and heading to the nearest ranger station."

None of them moved.

"Okay, this trip is fucking over," I hissed.

"Oh, come on, Raven. They're just playing a joke." Josh laughed. "We'll find them. I promise."

But I wasn't buying it. "This isn't a joke. I told you this trip needed to be taken seriously. We'll head out first thing in the morning. I suggest you have a talk with your group, Mr. Price. This is *not* how I run my trips with anyone. No exceptions."

I turned on my heels and stormed off to check on the rest of my supplies. Then I grabbed my canteen to fill with water. When I exited my tent, they were still standing in a huddle, talking too low for me to hear. I didn't give a shit. They could think I was overreacting all they wanted. There was no way in hell I was going to stay out here with someone who thought stealing gear was fun and games.

I headed down to the river, fuming, formulating my plan. I'd take them to the nearest station and demand my bonus, and they could find their own damn way home.

I stayed by the river for a long time, growing angrier when

Josh hadn't even come to check on me. I was even madder at myself for thinking I needed him to check on me.

On the positive side, at least I'd get to head home a bit sooner. I could maybe take the extra three weeks and go on a vacation for myself. That would be a nice change of pace.

# CHAPTER 12

## BEAR

STANDING ON THE RIDGELINE, I watched the two bears moving through the woods, heading straight toward me. If anyone else had seen it, they would have been terrified and confused at the same time.

It was strange, if not outright abnormal, to see a grizzly bear traveling side by side with a polar bear, especially in this part of Canada. I lowered my rifle as they approached, and I growled in greeting. The huge polar bear was Grant, and the grizzly was Cutter. Both bowed their heads and grunted back quietly.

"What do you have to report?" I asked.

Both bears took a step back and then stood on their hind legs. Their bones popped and snapped as they changed from large furry beasts into their human forms of Cutter and Grant.

Grant smoothed down his white hair while eyeing me. "Something's happening at the camp. The group cleared out after the woman went down to the river. I think something might have gone wrong."

My body stiffened. "What do you mean?"

"I mean she yelled at them, something about missing gear. She wasn't happy and looked like she was about to beat the shit

out of Price." Cutter smirked. "I wish she had. It would have saved us the trouble of knocking him the fuck out."

I glowered. "Or she would have gotten her hand bitten off. Missing gear?" I arched a brow. "They must have stolen it from her. I'm starting to get the feeling she's not part of the reason we're after Price."

Cutter and Grant nodded their heads in agreement.

"From the way they acted," Grant added, "they were really angry about her yelling. It showed quite a bit of disrespect, if she were one of them."

I concurred with his assessment. "No matter. We'll move in tonight."

Cutter glanced at me with a tilted head. "What's wrong?"

"What do you mean?" I replied.

"I can smell the uneasiness on you. Is it about the woman?"

I glared at him, even as my inner bear whined loudly in my head. The whining grew louder until I winced, fighting the urge to hold my head. Mercifully, after a while, it died down. I took a deep breath in through my nostrils, hoping the other two wouldn't notice, but from their wide-eyed stares, I knew they had.

"No, it has nothing to do with the human," I snapped. "Why do you ask?"

"Fuck, bro." Grant grabbed his bundle of clothes. "No need to get all ornery. It was just a question." He strode away without a backward glance.

Cutter snatched his clothes.

Grant was right. I was acting like a snappy asshole.

"Shit. I didn't mean anything by it."

"We just worry about you sometimes."

I glanced at Grant's back and then at Cutter. "Meaning what?"

"Meaning you're at your prime to find a mate, and you have yet to seek one out. The clan is worried about you, especially

your Aunt Kristine. We all just want to make sure your alpha bloodline continues, and the clan remains strong."

"Well, you all need to mind your own damn business," I snapped. "Get back to your positions. We'll move in soon enough."

Cutter stared at me long and hard until I snarled, "I'm fine, Cutter."

He raised a brow and snorted in reply, "Sure you are." He took a long sniff in the air. "Do you smell that?"

My head barely moved in acknowledgment as I stepped toward the south. The scent was there, just a hint in the wind. A herd of elk was moving through the area, not far from where we stood. I hadn't eaten all day, and neither had Cutter and Grant.

A snarl echoed around my head, and my teeth snapped in response. "Let's go," I told Cutter. "Before we take out Price and his group, it might be good to let the beasts feed."

Cutter grinned darkly and sprinted away after Grant, shifting mid-run. Then a large grizzly bear was lumbering through the trees.

Quickly, I removed my gear, stripping out of my clothes. The air was chilly as the sun was going down, but I barely felt the change in temperature. My skin was warm naturally from the beast raging within me.

Taking a step forward, the shift started to take over my body. A shooting pain raced through me as my inner beast rushed forth. Bones rearranged under my skin, expanding and stretching. The fur grew, covering my entire body, as my feet and hands spread and thickened. A few snaps of ribs later and a monstrous grizzly stood in my place, roaring in the night.

My dark chestnut fur rippled down my body in waves. Along my back were streaks of golden fur, a trademark of my bloodline, marking me as the alpha male of my clan. It was a position I had taken seriously for nearly ten years. When my uncle had passed, I had participated in the contest to become alpha, and I'd won over the rest of the males in my family. Since that night, I had

run my clan with a firm hand. The position was challenging but rewarding.

As bear-shifters, we were notoriously territorial and loners. We preferred to live in isolation from others, but bear-shifters were diminishing due to the females having breeding problems and wars with wolf-shifters over territory. So now, it wasn't uncommon for bear-shifters to live in clans under the leadership of an alpha to ensure the survival of our species.

Just a few years back, a run-in with humans had shown me how precarious our lives were. A member of my clan had been captured by a soldier near a base in the mountains. The soldiers hadn't known what to do with the man, who had been a bear only moments before. The clan had been in an uproar and ready to charge the base to get our brother back. However, I'd sworn to protect them, and I'd wanted to keep my word peacefully, if possible.

I had gone to the base, walking right up to the main road as a bear. As I'd gotten closer, I'd shifted into a naked man. At first, the soldiers had been prepared to shoot me, but the man in charge, General Harry Taggert, had stopped them. He'd gone out against the protests of his men and greeted me.

Together, we'd come to an arrangement that only men on that base would know about.

With Cutter, who was my second-in-command and beta, and Grant, who was my head enforcer, we had become part of a special task force, completing missions for the U.S. government under the most top-secret conditions they could manage. General Taggert had sworn to keep our existence secret, and he'd released my clan member.

Ever since then, I'd been going to the base every few weeks, despite the fact that my clan didn't trust the general even though I did.

In the beginning, I'd worried he'd go back on his word. I'd feared the government would raid my clan's lands and my whole family would be taken away, dissected, and killed. But General

Taggert never revealed to anyone that he had shifters working for him.

In the end, he'd turned out to be very trustworthy.

He'd even accepted an invitation to come to my home for dinner and meet a few clan members. Several of the cheekier clan members had tried to scare the general off, but he'd only laughed. He'd told them I was the only shifter he feared.

As two strong leaders, we'd built a trust over the years. It had been tested many times but had yet to break under the strain of secrecy.

My small team, Cutter and Grant, had been on over a hundred special missions, bringing in dangerous enemies, threats to the government and the country. In the beginning, we'd dealt solely with human targets, because Taggert hadn't known about the bigger threat—rogues, shifters that had refused to abide by the shifter code of conduct.

Then one day, General Taggert had called me and started asking questions about the existing number of bear-shifter clans and wolf-shifter packs. His question made me uncomfortable. It was one thing to reveal the existence of my clan but quite another to out other shifters.

As a member of the Shifter Council—a secretive group of leaders from various shifter clans and packs consisting of wolves, tigers, lions, and dragons—I was sworn to secrecy.

So I'd compromised, giving him the number of rogue wolf-shifter packs that had become a nuisance to shifters because of their reckless behavior of killing shifters and humans. But that was all the information I'd been willing to give him.

That was a few years ago, and soon after that first meeting, Josh Price had shown up on General Taggert's radar.

I'd already known about Price. Most shifters did. He was an alpha of a rogue wolf-shifter pack. Price showed little respect to other shifters and had flat out refused to abide by shifter law mandated by the council. The world was dangerous for shifters.

Our existence could easily be discovered if we didn't follow the laws that governed our conduct.

But Price felt he was above shifter law. Rumors had said Price was ruthless and ruled his pack by intimidation. When he'd come to power, he'd murdered quite a few males who he'd thought could challenge him for the alpha position.

When Josh had shown up on General Taggert's radar, Josh had been busy making a name for himself in many circles, and not in a good way. The local police had been cleaning up bodies, and they still had no idea where they'd come from. The corpses had been mutilated, and all the reports had pointed to the same cause of death—wild animal attacks.

But I'd known what was really going on, and my team and I were under orders to bring in Price and as many of his group, alive, as we could.

Seven against three wasn't bad odds, and I was always up for a challenge.

I ran through the trees, my big black nose sniffing the wind. Elk were definitely nearby, and my bear growled in anticipation of the kill. It had been cooped up for the past week while tracking Price. It was easier to hide as a man than as a giant grizzly bear, especially when Grant was a polar bear. That wouldn't be easy to explain away at all.

I caught up to Cutter and Grant, standing taller than both of them, as they waited for orders. I shook out my head and motioned for them to get a move on toward the elk.

We had just turned to head down to the valley floor when another scent hit my nose, and I stood on my hind legs, snarling.

*Wolves*, I grumbled through the mental link all shifters shared with their clans or packs.

Grant and Cutter stopped beside me.

*It's Price and his pack. They've shifted*, I explained.

*Do we move in?* Cutter asked. His bear growled and snapped his teeth, biting at the wind. As usual, he wanted a fight.

*We don't have a choice.* I fell back down to all fours and hurried through the woods.

We had been charged with finding Price, but there was another reason we'd tracked them this far north.

This was my territory.

Price in human form was fine on the land, but the second he'd shifted, he'd broken shifter law. I was now forced to act before Price could spill the blood of an innocent in my territory. Hunting animals was one thing—still disrespectful, but not against shifter law. If Josh spilled a human's blood, like the woman's, I wouldn't be taking him in alive. I'd have to kill him and the pack members he'd dragged with him.

When we reached the end of the valley, I shifted back to my human form and crouched low in the brush, trying to find Price and the others. The herd of elk was moving through the open field. My bear growled loudly in my mind, but I silenced him. There wasn't time to let my instincts take over—at least not yet.

I had to try to bring Price in still breathing. Otherwise, I'd have a lot more explaining to do with General Taggert.

I whiffed the breeze again and bent my head to the west. As I watched, I saw glowing eyes appear at the edge of the trees. My fingers turned to claws as they dug into the bark of a nearby tree, my beast growing angry at the sight of intruders in my territory.

They were all wolves. *But where is the woman?*

I heard footsteps crunch behind me. Then a growl turned into a human groan as Cutter came up beside me.

"Do we move in yet?" Cutter asked.

"No, we'll watch them. I don't want this to get messier than it has to be. This is our territory they're in. I'm hoping they know better."

"What about the woman?"

I wasn't going to prematurely charge in and risk my team for some stupid human. "She'll eventually find out who they are. Then maybe she'll get away."

"And if not?"

"We'll wait," I proclaimed, not bothering to directly answer the question.

*What will I do if the woman doesn't realize who she's with? Will I step in and save her?*

I'd caught her kissing Price, but that didn't mean she knew what she'd become involved with.

From this distance, I couldn't see much, but I knew she wasn't with them in the trees. I peeked backward to where their camp was, and my muscles involuntarily clenched. I had a sudden urge to run to her and protect her.

*I don't care about her. She's only a human.*

"Bear?" Cutter's voice pulled me out of my sudden daze.

I straightened. "Wait for my order to move in. Understand?"

Cutter nodded as I continued to watch the wolves at the edge of the trees, ready for them to make their move.

# CHAPTER 13

## RAVEN

After my confrontation with Price, I went to my tent, intending to stay there for the rest of the day, when he came by and asked, "Do you want dinner?"

Ignoring his question, I asked, "Did you figure out what happened to the gear?"

"You're the guide. Are you sure you even packed it?" he retorted.

My mouth tightened. "Go shove your fucking dinner up your damn ass."

When he walked away after trying to reason with me but failing, I lay back in my sleeping bag and gazed at the tent roof. I refused to speak with any of them until the next morning. When the sun came up, I'd be moving out—with or without them.

There was something in Josh's eyes when I'd asked him about the radio the first time. He'd lied to me. I wasn't sure why, but I could sense it.

*And if he lied about that, what else has he lied about?*

*And why did he take my communication devices?*

For most of the daytime, I could hear them running around the camp, but as the sun set, it became quiet. I paced back and forth inside my tent, wondering what I was going to do. Then I

decided I couldn't take it anymore. I grabbed my pocket knife, tucked it into my coat pocket, unzipped my tent, and then peeked out.

The campsite was empty. A large fire had been built up, and the huge flames reached nearly ten feet into the air.

*What are they trying to do? Burn down the tents?*

I rushed toward it and threw handfuls of dirt onto the logs to tamp down the hungry flames before it ignited the forest.

"Fucking idiots. Where did they go?" I mumbled, glaring around the empty site. *So help me God, if they get lost out here, I'm not sticking around to find their sorry asses.*

I couldn't hear them, and I didn't see a trail leading into the woods. There was no sign of them. It was as though they'd just up and disappeared.

Since the campsite was empty, I wasn't about to lose this chance to search for the radio and satellite phone. Josh had refused to do it, so he'd left me with no other option but to do it myself. I had no issues with going through people's things. Growing up in foster homes, I'd learned there was no such thing as privacy, especially when it came to having anything of my own.

I started with Boyle's and then Owen's tent, but I didn't find anything, so I moved on to Ian's and then Brian's tent nearby, and it was the same deal. I took a long glance around the campsite again before I unzipped Maggie's and then Brenda's tent and slipped inside. There was nothing in their tent either, but it smelled funny, musky almost.

"God, what is that wicked smell?" I wrinkled my nose. After taking a quick peek around, I left and went inside Josh's tent.

In the middle of it was a pile of blankets, almost like a nest. *Did he sleep curled up like that?* I stepped closer, the musky smell almost overpowering me in there, and gazed down at the covers. They were caked in black hair. The longer I stared at it, the more I realized it looked like dog fur. Halle had a large black dog, and her couch always looked like this. But Josh didn't have a dog with him.

I shook my head and kept up my hunt. I didn't have time for more questions. All I wanted was the damn satellite phone so I could call for the helicopter to come get me.

Josh's duffel was in the corner, and I rapidly poked through it. It didn't take long before I found the satellite phone and the radios buried underneath his clothes.

"What the hell? You bastard!" I yelled, pulling out the satellite phone.

I immediately dialed the local ranger station. It took a few rings before someone finally answered.

"Yes, this is Raven Holiday. I'm the guide with Josh Price's group. I need you to—"

The phone was ripped out of my hand.

"What the fuck?" I yelled.

Multiple hands reached into the tent and yanked me out by my shoulders and hair. My scalp erupted in pain, and the grasp on my shoulders dug in deep, nearly smashing the bone.

"Oh, hell no. Get the hell off of me."

I was dropped to the earth. When I glanced up, I found Josh and the rest of them glaring down at me. Josh held the satellite phone in his hands, and I watched as he crushed it to pieces, sprinkling them onto the ground in front of me.

I sat up and stared at the pieces and then back to Josh. "Who the fuck are you?"

"Were you trying to leave us, Raven?" he asked darkly, a growl under his words.

I tried to get to my feet, but Boyle shoved me back down.

"What are you doing? What is this shit? You can't keep me here!" I screamed, one step away from passing out.

"Oh, Raven," Josh crooned as he crouched down, running his fingers over my forehead.

I was still too stunned to move away.

"You are the chosen one," he told me. "So special in so many ways, and you have no idea."

I glared at him. *What is going on? Are they part of a cult?*

"First of all, I'm not a virgin, so if you want to sacrifice me for some weird ritual, it won't work." Josh glowered at my words, but I rambled on. "And second, I don't care what you guys are into. I am not going to be a part of it. I'm going to grab my gear, head to the ranger station, and get my ass home. You all can stay out here and be crazy on your own time."

I attempted to move again, but Boyle wouldn't let me.

"Get your hands off me, you asshole."

"She does have some fight in her." Boyle laughed, barely using any effort to keep me in place. "It's going to be a fun run this year, Alpha."

"Alpha? Are you kidding me?" I shrieked, relieved that he'd eased his hold, allowing me to get onto my knees.

"Be quiet," Maggie snarled. She lunged forward, making me fall backward. "Show respect, you filthy human."

I got back to my knees, trying to keep my fear in check even as I shook. "Human? We all are humans, you crazy bitch."

I gazed around at them with wide eyes as everything slowly began to snap into place.

*But that's impossible. There's no way... Just—no!*

But I'd seen their eyes, the way they'd hunted, the way they'd tracked me.

*Holy fucking shit.* I felt my mind beginning to close down.

"It's time. Bring her," Josh demanded before turning.

He walked away into the trees, and the rest of the group followed. Boyle seized my upper arm and yanked me to my feet. He dragged me along even as I tried to dig in my heels.

If they were going to kill me or sacrifice me or whatever, I wasn't about to go down easy. I fought against Boyle's grip until he finally became annoyed. He hauled off and smacked me across the face. It stung. I floundered and lost my balance, but Boyle didn't give me a chance to recuperate.

He pulled me along through the trees, but I didn't give up fighting. I clawed with everything I had, even threatened to bite him, when he raised his hand to strike me again. But a

harsh growl from Josh in front of the group stayed Boyle's hand.

I hadn't even noticed we'd come to a stop at the edge of the trees. Josh held up his hand, and the rest fell in beside him. Boyle dragged me to him, and Josh took hold of my other arm and twisted my face, so I stared down into the duskiness of the vale.

"What are we looking at?" I snarled. "Are you going to throw me down there or something?"

"No, Raven, you're not going to die—at least not yet."

"Oh, thanks. That's comforting," I grumbled.

He gripped my face harder and turned my back to the valley.

"I can't see anything. It's too dark. Just tell me already."

"Elk, a whole herd of them!" he shouted.

I shivered at the carnal tone of his words but kept a brave face. "Great. Can I go home now?"

He pinched my cheek, making me wince.

"You're going to watch and see what you humans are too blind to ever notice about your own world," Josh growled. "Tie her up."

"No. Let me go."

Boyle and Owen snatched me and pulled me back to a tree. They wrapped a rope around my upper body, tightly, pressing me back into the bark. I flinched and struggled to get loose, but it was taut. I was trapped. I gulped as I felt the biting cold of the night seeping deeper into my bones.

After a few minutes, I wasn't sure if I was shivering from the cold or from fear.

Josh stalked over to me and grinned. "You will watch and then you will understand."

"Understand what? That you guys are all psychos?"

Josh laughed darkly and then took a step back from me until he stood in line with the rest of them. Then they all stripped nude.

*Shit. Shit. Shit. I am in real fucking trouble.*

He didn't say anything, but he bent his gaze upward toward the nighttime sky. He shut his eyes, and a tremor ran down the length of his torso. I watched, transfixed, praying he was having a fucking seizure and would just drop dead, but what happened next made me curse and try even harder to get away.

Josh fell to all fours as his body became covered in black fur while loud snaps and popping filled my ears. His head transformed into that of a wolf, and he snarled at me, flashing sharp canines. He was tall at the shoulders with enormous paws, and for a second, I thought I was daydreaming.

Josh threw his wolf head back and howled. It sent chills racing down my spine, and I finally realized why I'd always felt the need to run away when I was near him.

He was a fucking werewolf. This crap rated a nine-point-five on my shit-o-meter.

I stared at him, amazed, despite the fear threatening to make me black out. The rest of them changed as well, shifting into massive killer beasts. They stalked toward me, growling and nipping at each other, until the wolf that was Josh howled again. He darted off, down to the valley floor, and the rest of them followed. From where I was, I could see them until they disappeared for just a moment before they popped back up near a herd of elk.

I was still in shock at what was taking place before my eyes. It wasn't possible. It couldn't be. Yet there they were. Seven humans had just turned into wolves—big, furry, probably-going-to-eat-me-later wolves.

*How the hell did I get trapped in this bloody nightmare?*

The satellite phone was broken, but the radios were still in the tent. All I had to do was get back there and contact someone, anyone, to come rescue me. Maybe, while they were busy, I'd be able to sneak off... But when I looked back toward the valley floor, I found I couldn't look away. Their bodies moved as one through the tall grass, downwind from the elk. The poor creatures had no idea what was moving toward them.

Part of me wanted to scream out, but that would probably just piss Josh off, and dealing with him in this wolf form wasn't something I could handle. For all I knew, he'd just rip me apart with his claws and be done with it.

Frankly, I wasn't sure why I was still alive. *Why had they revealed themselves to me? In fact, why the hell had they brought me out here at all?*

None of it made sense. I wasn't anyone special. There was nothing unique about me that should draw the attention of something supernatural.

But I was too distracted by what was happening below to spend much more time thinking about it.

The wolves moved in closer, and the moment the elk started to raise their heads and run, the pack lunged forward to attack. They moved in from two different angles and singled out a large elk.

Josh leaped forward, landing on the elk's back with a growl I heard from the top of the ridge. The elk screamed as Josh took it down. Then the other wolves moved in for the killing blow. The elk's throat was ripped out by one of their sharp canines, and blood spurted into the air. The scene before me was revolting, but I still couldn't look away.

As the rest of the herd raced away, I was left with the sounds of the dying elk, followed by the howls of the wolf pack. They tilted their heads back as one and let their voices carry through the wild.

"Jesus fucking Christ," I whispered.

Then I waited as they worked their way back upward to me, dragging the bleeding, broken elk body behind them.

# CHAPTER 14

## BEAR

*WELL, that answers that question,* Cutter rumbled through our mental link as Grant and I stood beside him. *Don't think she knew what they were.*

*Apparently not,* I replied tightly as my right eye twitched.

I growled, seeing the woman tied to a tree as she had been forced to watch Price and the rest of his small group turn right before her eyes. Then they had gone hunting, and even from this distance, I could smell the fear pouring off her, not that I could blame her. I could only imagine what was going through her head right then. At the same time, I was annoyed. She was lucky there weren't any other shifters around besides my group and Price's.

If anyone else had smelled her fear, it would draw them straight to her.

*Stupid humans. Always so fearful of what they don't understand.*

My bear whined and pawed anxiously at the ground. I was torn by what I usually felt for humans and this woman, this insane woman who had found herself alone in the wilderness with a pack of shifters.

*Do we move in?* Grant asked, yanking me from my thoughts.

*No, we'll wait. I don't want to risk this chance of catching Price,* I responded.

Price had killed an elk in our territory. Technically, that wasn't against shifter law, but if they shifted in front of a human unaware of shifters, killed the woman, or hurt her in any way, then I would have a vendetta against Price and his entire pack—not just those here, but those he might have left behind in my territory. It would start a war, something that hadn't happened between the shifters in decades, and I didn't have time to deal with that.

But if Price started it, I would be the one to finish it, no questions asked.

*Cutter, Grant, keep a close watch on the campsite,* I ordered. *I'm going to call home base and see if Taggert has any new information.*

*Might want to check back home, too,* Grant suggested. *Just in case things do go south.*

*Let's hope they don't,* I replied.

I made my way back through the trees. When I reached my gear, I shifted back into my six-foot-three human form and pulled on my gear. I tried to ignore the whining of my bear in my head. I kept thinking back to the woman and the fear on her face as she'd watched the wolves hunt and take down the elk.

Part of me wanted to run to her, rip the ropes off her body, and take her far away from here, from this nightmare.

But she was a human. I should have no feelings toward her whatsoever.

*So why won't the beast inside me shut up?*

It was acting as if she were a possible mate.

*Oh, fuck no. There's no way that's happening.* I was the alpha of the largest bear-shifter clan in North America and destined to mate with an alpha female shifter.

I ignored the inner beast, reaching my gear where I could get some sort of signal to call Taggert and then check in back home with the clan.

My home was located just on the border of Canada and

Montana, out in the wild where my family could roam freely without the fear of being spotted by humans. My territory was vast and had grown over the years from our clan making strategic land purchases.

It didn't hurt that my parents had built a lucrative billion-dollar business that had been passed on to me when they died. But it was getting harder to keep up with the demands of running the company, the needs of the clan, and my position on the council. Plus, there was always a lot of pressure on me to keep the peace with other shifters, especially the wolves. For centuries, there had been territory disputes, but for the last fifty years, peace had reigned between the families.

I wondered how long it was going to last. Price had to know he was in bear territory. *So why risk coming out here to hunt? Not to mention, why did he bring a human if they are trying to keep the peace?*

I radioed home base and told the man at the other end to connect me to Taggert. The soldier told me to hold on for a minute while he figured out where the general was. I waited impatiently as my bear clawed at the edges of my mind, begging to come out and go to the woman. The struggle made my head pound. It took everything I had to fight the instinctual need tearing up my gut.

*That damn woman.*

If it weren't for her, this mission would likely be over.

I needed to keep it together. *Maybe it's been too long since I had a good roll in the woods with another bear. Yes, that's exactly what it is.*

"Armstrong? Did you get Price yet?" General Taggert's voice came over the satellite phone.

"Not yet, sir, but we currently have eyes on him and his wolves."

"Why haven't you moved in yet? It's been over a week since I sent you out there."

I chewed my cheek for a second. I had to be careful how I played this. It wasn't that I didn't trust General Taggert. I just

didn't want to give away too much information about my kind and how we worked outside the laws of the normal government.

"We've run into a bit of a problem. I'm figuring out how best to deal with it."

For a long minute, there was quiet before General Taggert's rough voice came back along the communication channel. "Fine, deal with it however you have to, but I want this wrapped up sooner than later. Understood?"

"Yes, sir."

"So if you don't have Price in custody, why did you call?"

"Do you have any new information on Price? Maybe something that would explain a few more things about him?"

"Hmm, let me check," General Taggert mumbled. Some papers shuffled in the background, and he cleared his throat. "Actually, we do. We finally got permission to search his land in Nebraska, and... well, let's just say we found more than we'd bargained for."

There was a tightness in my chest. "Meaning what, sir?"

"We dug up a damn graveyard, that's what. Bodies everywhere, hundreds of them. There's no record of a cemetery ever being there and no sign of tombstones. They're still searching to see how many bodies there actually are. But," he added, "we did hear something interesting from our field guys."

I really hated when he did this—dragged out our conversations instead of just giving me what I needed. It was one of the general's tactics to try to get me to let something slip. I always had to be on guard when I talked to the damn man.

"And what's that?" I asked.

"The bodies were killed almost exactly a year apart from each other—at least the ones they've been able to check out so far. Strange, don't you think?"

More than just a question was in his tone, but I ignored it. My mind was too busy racing with the fact that this woman was in far more trouble than I'd originally thought. Killing her was

one thing, but if these bodies had all been killed about one year apart—

*Oh, fuck no. Is that what Price is doing all the way up here?*

"The Hunt," I hissed aloud.

"What was that?"

"Nothing, sir. Must have been static. If that's all, then I'll be signing off. I need to check with my men," I concluded.

I waited for General Taggert to either argue with me or let it go, and thankfully, he was either too tired to care or assumed I would fill him in later.

"Fine. But I want a full report the second Price is detained, Armstrong."

"Yes, sir," I retorted. Then I hung up before the general could ask anything else.

Pacing back and forth, I watched distant clouds roll in over the treetops. It was getting colder. The National Weather Service called for the temperature to drop and maybe even a bit of snow. It wasn't uncommon this time of year.

The bear in me growled in pleasure at the thought of snowflakes hitting my face, and then he immediately snarled when I recalled my conversation with General Taggert.

*The Hunt.*

It had been a long-standing tradition with shifters until moral-minded shifter leaders had finally taken control and put an end to it. It was against shifter law and punishable by torture and death if committed.

And here Price and his pack had been, continuing the ritual every single damn year. That was why they were this far north. It started to make sense. Price thought they were safe and could hide from the system. And he might have succeeded, too, if I had never become a part of General Taggert's team of special operatives.

I was in a tough spot. By shifter law, I could punish the wolves, kill them, and send the heads home as a warning to the

rest of his pack. Technically, they wouldn't be allowed to retaliate, but that didn't mean they wouldn't try.

And Josh's pack was large. He had family all across the Midwest, and I knew if one drop of wolf blood was spilled, they'd all come running. Wolves were ridiculous when it came to their pack members. They'd go on and on about revenge and serving out judgment. It gave the rest of the shifters headaches to listen to them bellyache about past slights.

I didn't even want to think about what Price's untimely death would bring out of the woodwork. All shifters were a bit on the crazy side, but wolves were the true psychos of the race.

I dialed another number and waited for it to be picked up. The minute it did, the sounds on the other end brought a grin to my face, warming my spirit.

"Bear? Why are you calling? Is everything all right?" my Great-Aunt Kristine asked.

The woman might be nearing three hundred years old, but she still sounded young. She would be the caretaker for the young bear-shifters when their parents were away on clan business. She would tell stories to keep our heritage alive in the younger generations, making us remember where we'd come from.

I shuddered because I wouldn't know what to do if I ever lost her, especially if we did begin a war with the wolf-shifters.

Pushing the dark thought aside, I responded, "Can you put Logan on the phone?"

"I haven't seen Logan in a week."

I grimaced.

Logan should have been home. He was one of my newest enforcers and eager to prove himself to the clan, so I'd sent him to Price's territory to do surveillance.

All shifters spied on each other. It wasn't a secret. It was how we kept each other in check.

"Has there been any news of wolves on the move?"

"Wolves, eh? Not that I'm aware of..." She paused. "Wait, why are you asking about wolves, Bear? And don't lie to me."

"I wouldn't dream of it, but I can't get into details."

"Hmm, well, I have heard more grumbling about that unruly Price pack. They found some more mutilated animal bodies a couple states over, and I hear humans are now getting very suspicious."

*Shit.* I ran my fingers through my hair. "Have you heard about anything strange happening in his territory?"

Screaming children in the background had my aunt yelling, "If you don't settle down, there will be no honeycomb cookies for dessert!"

Then there was utter silence.

"No. Nothing like that, Bear." She sighed into the phone before asking, "What's troubling you? You sound upset by something."

I leaned against a nearby tree as a few gentle snowflakes started to fall around me. They landed on my warm skin and melted instantly.

"It has to do with The Hunt," I whispered, as if afraid someone would overhear me. For a second, I felt like a damn little kid asking why curse words were bad and then being smacked on the knuckles for uttering them all out loud.

And my aunt's reaction was just the same. There was a sharp intake of breath, and I heard a door slam shut.

"Why do you talk of such dreadful things?"

"Because I believe it's still going on, Aunt Kristine. And I think I just found their next victim."

# CHAPTER 15

## RAVEN

I WAS STILL in shock when Boyle and Josh changed back into men. The rest stayed as they were, dragging the dead elk between them, as we headed back to camp.

Josh untied me and then shoved me ahead of him.

My hands curled into tight fists. "If you fucking shove me again, I'm going to kick your ass," I snapped.

He looked at my fists and just smiled, as if he'd love to see me try.

If it weren't for the fact that he was an animal, I would've taken my chances and fought for my freedom. But the horrific scene I'd witnessed with them taking down that elk had proven I was no match for their animal side.

I moved numbly, stumbling every few steps, as my mind tried to understand what had happened. Josh and his group weren't human. But my rational mind rejected the possibility. That shit just wasn't conceivable.

In fact, any second, I was going to wake up and realize this whole damn day had been a nightmare.

Then I faltered, fell, and hit my knee on a rock. It hurt like hell as the pain zinged up my leg.

"Shit!" I yelled as blood welled up in the rip of my jeans. "Dammit," I snapped.

Josh yanked me backward onto my feet.

"Can you give me a fucking second?"

He snarled. "No. Keep moving. We have a feast to get on with," he barked. "And you're going to watch."

I wanted to punch him in the damn face, but he seemed like the type of man who would actually enjoy the pain.

"You can't force my eyes to remain open," I argued as we reached the campsite.

Boyle started to build the fire back up to as hot as it had been before I'd gotten caught going through Josh's tent.

"I won't watch." My eyes narrowed.

Josh laughed as he shoved me forward, and I fell again with a curse.

"Yes, you will. You stand before one of the oldest shifter packs in the world, Raven, and you will watch in awe at our strength, our beauty, and especially our hunger."

I grinned for a second and then spit in his face. "Fuck off."

The other wolves were on me instantly. They pushed me flat onto my back in the mud. Their snapping teeth inches from my face, their foul breath smelled of blood and death. It filled my nose, making me gag at the rotten stench. Drool fell from their mouths and landed on my skin. It was hot and disgusting, but I was too busy watching their sharp teeth to be bothered by drops of spit.

"Enough. Leave her be," Josh thundered.

The wolves reluctantly backed up, then disappeared into the darkness.

Scrambling, I quickly sat up, backing away as far as I could until my back hit a tree. My heart thudded in my chest. My palms were sweaty, but I didn't flinch when Josh came toward me, still naked from head to toe.

His shaft was long and erect as he leaned in. He wrapped a hand around my neck, pulling my face up to meet his. I didn't

have a chance to brace myself before he pressed his lips against mine, trying to force his tongue into my mouth. Stubbornly, I refused to allow him entry, pressing my teeth together. He just laughed before licking my lips. I bit his lip to get him to back off and shoved against his chest.

"Damn," he yelled. Then he smacked me across the cheek.

I winced from the sting but kept quiet, refusing to give him the satisfaction of crying out.

"Fine, Raven. Have it your way. I was going to let you enjoy a little more fun before tomorrow night, but you don't appreciate my graciousness."

As he walked away, he nodded at Boyle. Boyle came over, rope in hand, and tied me to a tree once again.

If I was going to die, I fucking wanted to know why.

"What the hell are you?" I snarled. I struggled against the ropes, but Boyle had made them too stiff. I wasn't going anywhere. "Werewolves?"

Josh grumbled, "We are wolf-shifters. Werewolf was a name given to us by weak humans. It's an insult. Shifters own the night and the day."

I glanced behind him as the wolves pulled the elk all the way into camp, but none of them changed back to their human forms to eat.

I shuddered. *Are they going to eat it like that?*

"So what does that mean?" I needed to keep him talking. Just sitting there, listening to the wolves tear into the elk, made me sick. Talking would help keep me focused on something else.

"It means you have the honor of being in our presence. I'm over three hundred years old. Boyle here is my second-in-command and just a few years younger. He's repeatedly proven his merit, fighting by my side. The others with me are very important members of my pack. This isn't just a vacation for us. It is something so much greater than that."

Boyle grinned darkly as he stepped closer and licked his lips. I watched him shift back into the giant black wolf I'd seen

earlier. The scar he had as a human was even more terrifying on his wolf face. I fought against the ropes as he stalked forward, snarling and biting the air. I tried not to scream, but I couldn't stop the noise from bubbling up my throat and spewing loudly out of my mouth.

"Down, Boyle." Josh leered. "There will be time for that later. Now, let's eat."

Boyle turned and joined the rest of the wolves at the elk carcass.

Josh winked at me as I stared in horror. He shifted again, and with a loud howl, he dug into the elk flesh, ripping and tearing it apart into a bloody mess. I attempted to tune out the cracking bones and their guttural growls as they ate as one. It was revolting.

When I did glance over, I froze. There, beneath their jaws, was a vision of my lifeless body. I violently shook my head, and the elk reappeared under their chomping mouths, but the image stuck with me.

*Are they going to eat me next?*

# CHAPTER 16

## BEAR

I MADE my way back to Grant and Cutter, ordering them to shift back to their human forms. The two men stood before me, snowflakes falling on their naked shoulders, as they bowed their heads in respect to me, their alpha.

"So what did you find out?" Cutter asked.

"Not good news," I reported. "How's the woman? Still alive?" I'd tried to fight it, but the words had come out before I could stop them. My inner bear was the one who had demanded the question be asked.

Grant glanced sideways at Cutter before answering, "She's alive, bound to a tree, and breathing."

"Good. We need to move fast. She might not be alive for long."

"What do you mean?" Cutter demanded.

I stared at him. "The wolves, it seems, are still honoring the yearly Hunt, and the woman is their next victim."

"You've got to be shitting me." Cutter laughed. "There's no way they're that stupid!"

"They're wolves," Grant added with disgust written all over his face.

Cutter shook his head. "Yeah, but to come to another clan's

territory and then try to perform a Hunt? Is he trying to start a war?"

"I don't know, but the second it starts or when they kill her, I'll have no choice but to step in and take care of things our way."

"What will you tell Taggert?" Grant asked.

I sighed at his question. "I'll figure it out when the time comes. For now, we move in. If they're feeding, we might be able to catch them off guard. Let's go."

I started to yawn, which turned into a roar as I released my beast. Snow fell onto my fur and melted, cooling me in little bursts of chill. I peeked over my big shoulder as Cutter and Grant shifted.

Together, we made our way back through the woods to stop a bloody shifter war before it could start.

# CHAPTER 17

## RAVEN

THEIR FEEDING WAS GETTING to me. I couldn't drown it out any longer, and I knew the second I opened my eyes, I'd puke. I didn't have a weak stomach, but listening to them munching away on a corpse just feet from me was nauseating. Bile rose in my throat, and I tried to swallow it back down.

After a few deep breaths, I was all right until Boyle turned his wolf head toward me. His snout was covered with blood, and something was dangling from his teeth. It seemed to be a part of an intestine.

I turned my head seconds before everything came up. I heaved and coughed, getting it all out, even as I heard a man's laughter over my groaning.

Josh had shifted back to human form.

"Oh, Raven. You humans are so pathetic," he raged.

He leaned down as I spit up more vomit, and then I took a deep breath. It was a very bad idea. He reeked of death and blood and some other bodily fluids I really didn't want to think about.

"How can something so natural disgust you?"

"Eating a carcass raw is not normal," I snapped weakly. All

my energy had drained away from being in shock and getting sick. "That's revolting."

"Yes, well, we find humans equally disgusting."

"Really?" My eyes narrowed at him. "Thanks, you asshole."

"Now, Raven, don't be like that," he growled.

He painfully grabbed my shoulders and pulled me up onto my feet. My coat scraped the bark, but I was thankful it hadn't been my bare skin. I was still tied to the tree, but at least I was standing. My feet had fallen asleep, and the sharp tingle helped keep me focused.

"You get a chance to be a part of history here," he said.

That really got my attention. I shook my head and asked, "What the hell are you talking about?"

He grinned, and his canines grew to their wolfish size. "The Hunt, my dear, sweet Raven. You get to be part of The Hunt."

"The Hunt? What the fuck is that?" I asked sharply even though I had a feeling I knew already.

"It is a most sacred tradition that many of the packs feel is outdated"—he shrugged—"but not me. I have kept the tradition going for years, and I will continue to do so with you. After all, it is the natural order of things. It's the reason we still exist at the top of the food chain." He gripped my chin hard between his thumb and index finger. "Your blood, your beating heart, will give us strength and empower us all."

I glanced upward toward the stars, but they were covered over by clouds. A light snow was falling. It was getting colder by the hour, but I hadn't noticed with being so close to the roaring fire.

I didn't want to be here.

I wasn't ready to face this horrible reality.

When I glanced back down, Josh was still there in front of me, and the wolves were crunching away on the bones of the elk, sucking out the marrow. It was loud enough to almost make me sick again.

*Fucking animals are going to make me go vegan again.*

When I was sure I wasn't going to puke once more, I fumed, "What do I have to do with any of this?"

Josh reached out and held my face. "Good to see you still have that fight in you. You're going to need it come tomorrow night."

"Tomorrow night?" I squeaked.

He leered, pressing his naked body against mine. I grimaced and tried to pull away, but there was nowhere to go. I could tell he enjoyed it, that he wanted to keep pressing himself against me. A growl started deep in his chest and reverberated through my body. His manhood was hard against my thigh, and all the good feelings I'd had earlier about him seemed like nothing more than a prelude to this hellish nightmare.

He licked my cheek. "I know you feel the heat between us. There could be so much more, but sadly, you're not a shifter, and I don't mate with fucking humans."

I gagged at the word "mate" and tried to push him away the best I could. "Get the fuck off of me, you bastard. Let me go. I won't tell anyone what I saw. I swear it. Just let me get out of here."

"Oh, you will get out of here, my pet. Don't you worry."

"What are you talking about?"

Josh snapped his fingers, and the rest of the wolves quickly shifted back into their human forms. They were covered in blood from head to toe, and their eyes glowed amber in the firelight. They took a step forward, and I flinched without meaning to. Josh noticed and smirked.

"It's time to explain the rules before we leave you to make peace with your destiny," he drawled.

My stomach plummeted. "Rules for what?"

"The Hunt you are about to be part of. You see, hunting animals is only so much fun for us. But hunting humans... Well..." He smiled. "That's been somewhat of a decadent luxury for our kind for centuries. A sort of ritual," he revealed, running his fingers down my cheek.

I jerked my face away.

He grabbed my chin again, forcing me to look at him. "Tomorrow morning, we'll cut you loose and give you a two-day head start. If you can make it back to the States, you'll win, but if not, we'll catch you, and... well..." He turned his gaze to the half-eaten elk carcass, then back.

I gulped. There was something dark in his eyes, but I was too frightened to understand what it was.

"You're going to hunt me?" I croaked. "Like a fucking animal?"

Josh laughed coldly. "What can I say? Humans give us more of a challenge. It's quite exciting," he replied, as if we were discussing going to a baseball game. "But there will be enough time for you to figure out what you're going to do. For now, get some sleep, my beautiful prey, for tomorrow you must run for your precious life."

My legs felt like jelly. "I don't understand. Why?" I whispered in shock. "I've never done anything to you."

"To me personally? No, but there are others..." He stopped himself and grimaced. "But you will learn all about that later. For now, just know your death will bring about the greatest event in shifter history and help us with the ritual that drives our pack." Such a tone of finality was in his words.

This crazy motherfucker actually believed if they didn't go through with this *Hunt*, they would all die.

That would be just fine by me.

"Rest now, Raven. Sleep peacefully."

*No. No. No.*

I tried every way to rationalize what was happening, but it didn't work. No matter how much I wished myself to be somewhere else, I was still tied to this fucking tree, and Josh was a werewolf—no, a shifter. And this was his pack.

I watched as they all turned back into wolves before they ripped apart what was left of the elk carcass.

I shuddered. Those teeth... they'd use them to tear me apart.

I was going to be sick again, but I forced myself to breathe deeply and focus on staying alive.

My hands were by my pockets, so I could at least keep my hands warm while I tried to figure out a plan. I was still standing, and being upright helped me keep the urge to pass out at bay.

I waited patiently for them to be distracted, and I tried not to smile with delight when they all disappeared from the campsite. Their bloodcurdling howling echoed around the woods, but it grew farther and farther away.

*Finally. Maybe I can get the hell out of here.*

I pushed my hands into my pockets and felt something cold in the left one. *My pocketknife.* I stretched my fingers, feeling the metal in my hand.

"Thank God. A bit of luck for me," I whispered.

Keeping my eyes pinned to the woods where they'd disappeared, I slowly reached my arm up and started to saw away at the ropes. They might have been too tight to move my body, but I could move my arms enough.

*Idiots. Did they really think I was so pathetic that I wouldn't try to escape?*

As it was, I had to cut the ropes inch by painful inch. I kept my breathing steady as I would on all my adventures, and I told myself that was exactly what this was—just another adventure.

I'd make it through this shit. I could survive in the woods and figure out a way to get back home. As long as I headed south, I'd be fine and make it to the States.

The contract with Josh was for a month. We were already a good chunk of the way into the trip, and if I didn't check in soon, someone would send help.

*Yeah, Halle will make sure I'm okay.*

I shifted my right shoulder and then my left, and I almost let out a cry of triumph before I caught myself. The ropes were loose enough. Quietly, I slipped out from under them and made my way, walking backward, into the tree line.

None of the wolves appeared in the campsite, and no eyes

glowed in the darkness nearby. They were too busy howling at the moon and probably hunting more elk. After a few more steps and then a few more, I turned and sprinted deeper into the forest. I didn't pay attention to where I ran. I just blindly took off into the darkness.

*This is insane.*

I just needed to find help, any help.

I ran and ran. My chest burned from breathing in the cold air, but I forced myself to keep going. We weren't too far from the river. If I could make it there tonight, then at least I'd have fresh water.

*Would they lose my scent if I crossed it?*

Part of me doubted it, but it was worth a try.

I slid to a stop in the mud and froze.

"You've got to be shitting me," I groaned in horror as a hulking form came out of the shadows.

I gulped and took a few hesitant steps back, but it was too late. The monstrous beast had seen me and headed my way with a quick lumbering gait. With my heart hammering and my blood thundering away in my ears, I was surprised I was still on my feet.

The bear turned completely around, staring into the forest. It stood on its hind legs and roared in fury. I had a second to notice the strange markings on the bear's back before it circled to face me, locking eyes on me.

It was the bear from my dreams.

When it trudged closer to me, I scrambled back too quickly, falling onto my ass. The huge bear snarled in my face.

*Oh, damn. He's going to eat me.*

I nearly pissed on myself when it sniffed my neck. Then it barked once, a small huffed sound.

"Please," I pleaded.

Then I stopped dead when its coarse tongue licked my neck.

*Holy shit.*

My limbs shook, and darkness consumed me.

# CHAPTER 18

## BEAR

GENTLY, I nudged her with my paw and then my nose, but she didn't move. Instinctively, I inhaled deeply to investigate her scent just as I would with anyone I'd met for the first time.

*Fuck.*

The tantalizing combination of vanilla and cinnamon raced up my nostrils and shot straight to my bulging erection, making it jerk.

My bear growled his arousal, wanting to investigate her mouthwatering scent further.

*Damn. She's trouble.*

I started to back up to beat a hasty retreat, and then I stopped dead in my tracks, rooted to the spot. She was going to freeze to death if I left her in the mud. With one last glance around to ensure I was alone, I shifted back into a man and scooped the woman up into my arms.

The second I glanced down at her face, my heart skipped a beat. Not only was I drawn to her exotic beauty, but I was also strangely driven to protect her.

*Absolutely beautiful.*

*Mine,* my bear growled.

*Fuck no,* I hissed back.

The long, dark curls that escaped her bun compelled me to run my fingers through them. Her skin was the color of hot chocolate. Her pouty lips begged to be repeatedly plundered. Her perfect hourglass figure made my loins swell.

*Damn, she's the full package.*

Snowflakes fell onto her cheeks and long black eyelashes but didn't wake her. I could stare at her all night, and I probably would have if I hadn't remembered where we were. Just holding her in my arms sent my gut twisting and heart pounding. My beast growled in satisfaction, but I growled back with irritation. There was no time for a battle of wills.

I knew of a nearby small cave where she would at least be out of the elements and away from Price and his men until she awoke. I'd get her there and then be on my way. That was all I would do for her.

Despite what my beast thought, she was not my mate to protect.

But minutes later, as I was about to leave her in the small cave, I felt the strong primal urge to stay and keep her warm, and then she groaned and rolled over.

*No. I have to go.*

Quickly, I left the cave and shifted back into my bear.

# CHAPTER 19

## RAVEN

I HAD enough energy to lift my head for a moment, and I saw the shadow of a bear lumbering away. I didn't register where I was or why a bear was there. I was dreaming. It was all just a dream.

Darkness overtook me, and I gratefully sank back into it, but then the howling of wolves echoed through the night, and I shot straight up. My heart thundered away in fear.

*Have they found me already?*

I wrapped my arms around my legs, tucked my head down so I couldn't see or hear, and prayed to God I'd still be alive come morning.

## CHAPTER 20

### RAVEN

I HEARD SOMETHING EARSPLITTING. I thought I was dreaming, but then I jumped as the noise grew too loud for me to ignore. It was my teeth chattering.

The cave had given me some shelter throughout the night, but I was still cold. I was fortunate I had my coat and boots, but I didn't have gloves or thermals. The cave wasn't going to keep me warm if the temperature kept dropping. Judging by the weather I'd seen before, that was very likely to happen. I had no other choice. I had to make a plan, any plan, and get out of the cave.

I needed to move.

Hours had passed since I heard any howling, but that didn't mean anything. Running away last night had apparently jumpstarted the rules. There was no more two-day head start. The Hunt had begun early, and I wasn't prepared.

The sun was barely up. The light outside the cave was pale and thin from heavy cloud cover, but at least it had stopped snowing. My limbs ached from my run through the woods, but I forced myself to stretch them out. I had to figure out which direction was south and then move as fast as I could without wearing myself out too quickly.

This was truly going to be a test of my survival skills.

After stretching, I groaned when my muscles protested. Crawling out of the cave, I was careful to check my surroundings. There were no footsteps in the mud, human or wolf.

*But are those bear tracks?*

"Maybe it wasn't just another dream." I reached out and measured my hand against the print.

Before I'd passed out, come to, and then crawled into the cave, I'd seen a bear, but I'd thought it was a figment of my imagination. It was the logical explanation anyway. But those bear tracks were huge, bigger than any I'd ever seen.

I pulled my hand back and stood. There would be time to think about that later. I needed to move and get somewhere safe. I checked the trees around me, looking for moss. The moment I found some, I turned the other direction until I was facing south, the route that would take me back to the States.

My pace was steady, plowing through the snow-clad trees. The last thing I wanted to do was sprain anything. I kept my gaze down to avoid any sticks or rocks, and I watched out for dips. The snow cover was only a few inches, but from the look of the clouds overhead, more would be coming by nightfall. My breath created little white puffs as I went. The air burned my lungs, so I forced myself to slow down.

It was definitely colder than it had been the past few days. I rubbed my arms and kept them close to my middle, but it did little to keep away the chill. There was a tear in the knee of my jeans and a draft blew right up my leg.

"Damn." I stopped to see if there was a way I could fix it.

But the tear was pretty large. I had no equipment with me to repair my jeans—at least nothing that would help. Hell, I didn't even have my gloves. I'd be lucky if I didn't wind up with frostbite.

At some point, I'd have to find shelter and fresh water, along with something to eat. But water had to come first. I could last a few days without food, if need be. Warmth was another neces-

sity, but I'd have to be careful with the fire. I wasn't sure how Josh Price and his pack would track me during the day.

*Do they only turn at night? How does being a wolf-shifter even work in the real world?*

"Guess I should have paid more attention to those damn frightful movies," I whispered. "Maybe I would have learned something useful."

The thought kept me amused. The more I kept my thoughts positive, the better off I'd be. I knew the real horror of my situation hadn't really sunk in yet. I was being hunted. In the light of day, it seemed like a bad dream. There was no howling or dead elk bodies torn to shreds surrounding me.

All that blood... there'd been so much of it.

I suddenly stopped and turned to the side to vomit, but all I did was dry heave. Everything else had come up last night. I leaned against a tree as I wiped my mouth on my sleeve and took a few deep breaths to calm my stomach. I felt weak, shaky, but I didn't have time to just stand there and hope they wouldn't find me.

It was up to me to get out of this mess. I needed to head south, find a phone, and call for help.

*I will make it. I will survive.*

# CHAPTER 21

## BEAR

THROUGH MY SCOPE, I watched the human get sick, and my bear grunted as my right eye twitched almost nonstop.

He wanted to go to her, comfort her, protect her, but I told him to shut the fuck up. We didn't have time for that. I'd saved her last night and gotten her out of harm's way. That was all I was going to do for her, nothing more. She was on her own.

My focus had to be on Price and his wolves.

"How's she doing?" Grant asked, coming up behind me.

"Why do you care?"

"Because, obviously, you do—a lot."

I glared at him and growled until Grant shrugged and walked off.

"Where's Cutter?" I asked.

"Tracking. We lost Price and his pack scent a few miles back. He's trying to pick it up again."

"Which direction?"

Grant pointed, and we headed off. I could still smell the woman as I followed Grant through the trees. I'd keep tabs on her. I wasn't sure why, but I had a feeling she'd eventually lead us to Price—or he would catch up to her in the end. Whether she lived or not was the other question. It wasn't that I wanted to

use her as bait, but if it got me Price and the others, that was what I'd use her for.

I had a personal vendetta against him and his pack.

They were trying to perform a *Hunt*. If we didn't stop his pack before they killed her, I'd have to kill them all, and that would start a war. Shifter law was much more brutal than human law, and the alpha—not his family members—always carried out the sentence. If Price needed to be executed, I would be the one to do it.

I wasn't going to stain anyone else's hands with blood.

We needed to touch base back home again and make sure they were watching the rest of the wolves.

I told Grant to keep moving on and that I'd catch up. I pulled my satellite phone out of my vest and dialed the main house. It was morning, so Aunt Kristine would be busy with the children, as their parents had been dropping them off for the day.

The phone rang a few times before a gruff voice finally answered, "Bear? Is that you?"

"Yeah, Kyle, it's me."

Kyle was my youngest nephew, barely out of college and starting to take on more duties within the clan. If anything happened to me, Cutter, or Grant, he'd be the one the clan fell to. I put a lot of responsibility on the younger bear, but there might come a day when I didn't come home, so Kyle would need to be ready.

"Catch me up on what's happening there," I stated.

"What did you do to piss off the wolves?"

I snarled. "Why?"

"Reports have been coming in since early this morning. They're on the move."

Children were yelling, and Kyle told them to hush up. That was followed by loud growling and more screams. I could just picture my large nephew, half-shifting so his bear head appeared to scare off the youngsters terrorizing him.

"Cars have been heading to Price's house every few minutes. And they're not just coming over to visit. Most of the wolves are armed."

In agitation, my claws grew and I dug them into a nearby tree, trying to contain my anger.

*How have things escalated so quickly? Or does this have to do with something else?*

"I need you to stay on top of this. Let me know if they start to head north."

"There's something else, Bear. The Shifter Council has called a meeting. They've requested all pack alphas and clans to be there."

"Someone else might have to go in my place if we can't wrap up this mission first. Price is my priority right now. Has Logan come back yet?"

"No, I haven't seen him."

"Shit." *Something is terribly wrong.* "Okay. Report to me every two hours with news on what's happening in our territory and with the wolves. Is that understood?"

"Yeah. What's going on?"

"Nothing you need to be concerned about," I countered. "Don't forget to call me."

I hung up and hurried to catch up to Grant, who was already speaking quietly with Cutter. It sounded like they'd found something.

"What do you have?" I asked.

"You want the bad news or the very bad news first?" Cutter asked tightly.

I just stared at him before rumbling, "I don't have time for this shit, Cutter."

"Okay. Relax, bro," he muttered. "They're tracking the woman, but she has a good head start. They seem to be abiding by the age-old rules and are in human form right now. They won't shift again until nightfall."

"A minor advantage for her. What's the other news?" I asked.

"A blizzard's moving in. About twenty miles out. It'll be here in a few hours."

My gut clenched, and I immediately turned toward her direction. She wouldn't last through a blizzard—at least not without help. "You two keep tracking Price and his group. I'm going to keep an eye on the woman."

Cutter and Grant exchanged a glance, and Cutter nudged him a few times with his elbow.

"You sure that's a good idea?" Grant finally asked.

"We've already decided to use her as bait. I'm going to watch her closely and hope Price and the others close in."

My blood boiled with anger at the thought of seeing the woman in Price's grip and hearing her screams of fear again. Last night, when Price had touched her, rubbing against her, it had taken everything in me not to go barreling through the campsite, claws ready to slaughter them all without question.

My bear whined, and I snarled aloud, trying to keep it in check. I took a deep breath of air and cursed. I could smell her, even from this distance.

*Why did it matter?*

She was just a fragile human who'd gotten in the way. She wasn't worth my time, and I certainly didn't have feelings for her.

*So why wouldn't my bear give me a damn break and shut the hell up?*

I needed to be alone to try to deal with my thoughts. "You and Grant head out. I'll be in touch soon."

They undressed and stashed their clothes. With the loud popping of bones, their bodies shifted into their massive bear forms before they moved off into the trees.

My booted feet stayed planted where they were as I tried to sort out my jumbled thoughts. I felt like a cub again, unsure of what steps to take next. I needed to get back to home base and deal with the wolf issue from there, but I couldn't leave Price out here. General Taggert had sent us on a mission to capture Price and his pack.

I'd never failed a mission before, and I wasn't going to start now.

Besides, the bear growling inside me told me he wasn't about to leave the woman to her fate either. Plus, if I left her now, I'd never be able to deal with the guilt. She'd probably be killed in the most brutal fashion possible.

I shuddered.

When The Hunt first had come about, shifters wouldn't just kill the humans they'd brought along. They'd torment them for days. It was all a part of the old tradition—conquering the humans, making them feel as if they were the animal. They would beat her, burn her, and possibly skin her, as some clans and packs used to do. Then, to end it all, they'd cut out her heart and eat it, absorbing her spirit, and then bathe in her blood to completely become one with their kill. It empowered them as a group, gave them strength with each passing year. The idea was to take on what made their enemies stronger and add it to the shifters' form.

At least that was what the old stories alleged.

It wasn't true, though. It was plain brutality and nothing more.

The horrific tradition had finally been outlawed.

I'd assumed all shifters would follow the law. Nowadays, most tried to fit in with humans to keep their kind safe and hidden from society. But apparently, Price thought that was beneath him. His pack, it seemed, had never stopped The Hunt.

A harsh scent hit my nose, and I froze.

*Smoke? Why is there smoke?*

"She built a fire? The idiot," I snapped, charging forward through the trees. My bones cracked and reformed as I shifted mid-run. My clothes fell from my huge fur-covered body, and I hurried through the trees, hoping to find the woman before the wolves did.

# CHAPTER 22

## RAVEN

I WAS COLD ALREADY, but I knew it was going to get worse. The clouds were growing darker in the distance. A storm was coming, and if it snowed before I could find shelter and get warm, I'd be dead by morning.

I'd been following the stream for a while, mostly to have access to water, but I'd pulled away from it, looking for a place I could build a fire. The last thing I wanted was for Price and his pack to see smoke, but a fire would be the only way for me to get warm unless I found a cabin way out here in the middle of nowhere.

I wasn't even sure where exactly I was. I had no idea where the camp from last night was. My feet had just taken me as far away and as fast as possible. That meant I could've run in any direction. Following the stream was the only real guide I had.

Already, I'd lost track of time, and I only knew the sun would be setting soon. With it would come a storm I wasn't prepared to face.

A ridgeline was ahead, stretching high above me.

"Perfect," I whispered.

On my way there, I started to gather sticks, large and small, for kindling. At least I knew how to build a fire without any aid.

Otherwise, I'd freeze to death. But maybe that would be a good thing. I'd be dead before they had a chance to rip apart my body. There would be no pain, nothing but sweet darkness. I wouldn't be cold any longer.

*Wait, do I want to die? Am I really just going to give up like that?*

I stared at the wood in my hands and angrily threw it onto the ground.

*The hell I am.*

I'd get out of here, or I'd go down swinging.

I built up the wood, making sure the fire would be close enough to the face of the cliff so the smoke would rise up against it and then dissipate. Then I found some dried leaves and brush, piled it together, and started working on getting a fire going. It wasn't the easiest way, but I didn't have any flint.

After half an hour, I finally got one going. It was small, but with a few gentle breaths and the right amount of kindling, I was able to keep a steady flame, and I slowly built the rest of the wood around it.

As my fingers felt warmth seeping back into them, I tried to relax and savor the feelings. Heat all over felt so good I almost fell asleep right then, but I forced my eyes to stay open. The fire gave me comfort at least, even if only for a little while, but I knew I couldn't stay there too long. The cliff provided me some protection, but not enough. I'd have to find something hidden and out of the way.

Once I'd warmed up enough to actually feel my limbs again, I got up and started to look around for anything that might get me out of the elements.

Keeping the fire in sight, I made my way around the base of the cliff, but I saw no crevices to crawl into until I gazed up. About ten feet from the ground was a small cave-like opening. If I could get up there and cover the opening with something, I might be able to stay out of sight for a while.

I looked around for footholds and managed to climb up enough to peer inside. It appeared empty. At least there were no

animals. I'd heat some stones, find a good-sized branch that wouldn't look out of place across the entrance, and then hide out there until morning.

Maybe then I could come up with a better plan of keeping myself alive.

## CHAPTER 23

### BEAR

I CREPT THROUGH THE TREES, staying in bear form, as I spied. She built a fire, and the clever woman was using the cliff to hide the smoke.

*Damn, maybe she's not some helpless human.*

I hunkered down while observing her build up the flame and warm herself. The fire crackled, and for a moment, she looked like she was going to fall asleep, but then she jerked herself up and started walking around.

*What is she looking for?*

My growl rumbled deep into my chest as I tried to figure out what she was doing when I saw her start to climb up the cliff into a dark crevice.

For the next hour, I closely watched her while she warmed several large stones in the fire and then found a brush. She removed her coat and carefully moved the stones, one by one, up to the crevice. Then she dumped dirt over the fire and pulled the large branch up behind her, completely covering the opening to the crevice.

If I hadn't seen her go in, I wouldn't have known she was there—well, besides smelling her scent that was driving me

insane. I wanted nothing more than to go to her, curl up beside her, and keep her warm.

*No, we're not doing that,* I argued with my inner beast.

My bear growled and snarled, but I kept him in check.

Snow started to fall, and I glanced up at the sky, my black nose sniffing the air. The storm was close, almost on top of us. At least she'd been smart enough to get out of it.

But the sun was going to set, and the wolves would be coming out.

The snow started to come down harder as the wind picked up. The second the sun sank below the ridge, a howl echoed through the woods.

The wolves were on the hunt.

I glanced around. I had to keep them away from this spot, and I had to make sure they wouldn't figure out where she was. I got off my haunches and started to use my large paws to mark up any prints left by the woman's boots. Then I stomped all over what remained of her fire.

There had to be no signs she was here at all.

## CHAPTER 24

### RAVEN

I CURLED up around the hot stones. The warmth gave me some comfort as I pressed myself as far back into the crevice as I could.

Maybe it was stupid to hide here. They'd find me, and then I'd be trapped with no way out.

Fear gripped me when I heard something moving through the brush just outside.

*Have they found me already?*

I'd heard the howling and instantly curled up into a tighter ball, as if that would save me, but what I heard sounded bigger than a wolf.

Curiosity got the better of my common sense, so I scooted forward enough to see around the branch I'd covered the entrance with. A gust of wind blasted snow into my face, but I was still able to see the large animal shuffling around the base of the cliff. It was definitely covered in fur, with strange markings on its back, and it was bigger than a wolf.

Then I froze. It was the bear from my dreams. When the bear turned, I gasped and then quickly covered my mouth with my hand.

The bear was real. What was worse was I'd seen it right after running away from Price.

*How can this be?*

*And more importantly, has it been following me?*

But that was ridiculous. Bears didn't follow people, let alone stomp out the remnants of fires, as it was doing now. It raised its large head, and I allowed myself to study it for a few minutes more. It was a handsome creature with a large head and silky-looking fur. It was probably warm under all that hair.

I could just imagine curling up underneath it and letting the coldness leak from me, replacing it with glorious waves of heat.

I sighed at the thought, studying the rest of the bear. Its eyes were dark, but when they turned away from the shadow of the cliff, I swore I saw a glint, one like Price and the others had.

I scrunched back into the crevice as my palms grew sweaty, despite the cold. *If it was following me, could there be more of them, different creatures?*

No, I didn't want to think that. It was hard enough to believe wolf-shifters were out there, let alone other creatures that could easily tear me into shreds, creatures that could think like humans because they were humans.

*If the bear is a shifter or whatever, why is it following me? Why not catch me and kill me?*

That seemed to be what Price and the others planned on doing.

*So what's this bear doing?*

The wolves howled again, and I forced myself to worry about my current problem. Besides, the bear seemed to know I was there and didn't seem interested.

*Because it's just a bear*, I forcefully reminded myself. That was what I told myself over and over. *It's just a bear, nothing more. There isn't anything else for me to worry about—no other shifters and no other packs on killing sprees, wanting nothing more than to eat me alive.*

I pulled the stones closer to me, surrounding myself in the dying warmth I knew wouldn't last through the night. The

stones were a trick I'd learned during a survival tactics class. I was lucky I'd paid enough attention to the intricacies of this trick.

But at that moment, I would've given anything to be back in my comfy apartment, snuggled under my comforter, watching reality shows, with a glass of my favorite wine in one hand and a huge bowl of popcorn in the other. Instead, I'd found myself smack dab in the middle of my own private reality show nightmare with a very slim chance of getting out alive.

As my eyes started to close from exhaustion, I found myself picturing a different life.

*What if I'd settled down with one of those rich men I took on trips?*

He'd have to be my type, with dark hair, a chiseled jaw, and a pair of big, strong calloused hands. I shivered as I thought about those hands sliding over my dark skin. He'd also have to love the outdoors, nature, and lots of adventure.

I smiled.

What if I'd been able to stop working and just enjoyed life? Having children had always been a distant thought, especially since I'd been abandoned so young and didn't know shit about family, but part of me believed I'd be a good mother. I was nurturing, loving, and thrill-seeking.

Shit, not many children could say their moms jumped out of airplanes or climbed mountains or explored the darkest depths of caves. My parents might have given me up, but I'd sworn long ago if I decided to have children, I'd always be there for them, every fucking day, no matter what life brought.

Now I might never get to know.

Halle and my bosses might never even find my remains if I froze here in this crevice or if Price and his pack caught me and ate me alive.

My existence would simply fade away.

No one would mourn my passing besides Halle. My bosses would miss me simply because of the loads of money I'd brought in, but beyond that, they wouldn't give a shit.

"I swear, if I get out of this fucking mess alive, I'll make it priority number one to find a good man to settle down with, and we'll have a shitload of babies."

My eyes shot right back open after an image of that poor elk had flashed through my mind. All my training, and none of it could've prepared me for this crap.

*Dammit. Where was the How to Fight Off Wolf-Shifters class when I needed it?*

"Why couldn't I have been a nerd?" I whispered before tucking my face into my coat and praying for warmth and the blizzard to stop.

Snow blew in through the branch. It wasn't much, but by morning, I could be half buried alive. The thought made me colder as I forced the tears to stay away, squinting my eyes shut until it hurt.

"Don't cry, Raven," I fiercely reminded myself. "You never fucking cry—ever."

But even as I scolded myself, a single tear slid down my cheek and froze before it could hit the ground.

# CHAPTER 25

## BEAR

I FINISHED COVERING up her tracks and then headed up the ridge so I would have a clear view of the area. I hid my bulk within the trees and waited. The air was bitterly cold, but I couldn't feel it underneath my three layers of thick fur. Snow started to cover me, and I let it. It would be best to blend in and not let the wolves know exactly where I was.

They'd be able to smell me, but I wanted them to.

I wanted them to know they were being watched.

I wanted them to know they weren't the only hunters out for their prey tonight.

I waited impatiently. I knew they would follow her scent. It wasn't that hard to find—at least not for me. Her scent had been stuck in my nose since the day she stepped foot into my territory. My bear couldn't stand being away from her, and I had to admit my human side was slowly starting to admire her for surviving. She hadn't run or screamed in terror through the woods. She was being smart, using her wits. It was a quality few humans possessed.

A twig snapped somewhere in the absolute quiet of the snow falling around me. My claws dug into the snow and mud beneath me as I waited to see who would appear. At first, all I saw were

eyes glowing in the darkness. One pair, then two, and three, but then no more. They'd split into groups. Typical wolves, they never hunted alone.

*The cowards.*

They sniffed the air, and one howled.

Even from where I was, I felt the woman's icy fear.

I hoped she'd stay quiet. The last thing she needed to do was make any sort of noise and draw them in closer. The small clearing was filled with my scent. I hoped it would be enough to scare them off.

The three wolves edged in, yipping at each other, trying to coax the other forward to investigate. The large black one finally growled at the other two and stepped around them. Its massive body was solid muscle, and even from my spot, I could see the long, jagged scar running across his face.

*Boyle.*

That was one wolf I knew well, mostly from reputation and because he'd gained that scar from one of my relatives. It was a story my aunt would still tell the cubs while around a fire at night.

Boyle had wandered into bear territory as a human and spotted an attractive woman walking through the woods. The woman was a bear-shifter, and Boyle had known it. He'd tried to flirt and coax her into kissing him, but she'd refused. He'd taken it as an insult and started to attack her. Before she could shift, he'd knocked her unconscious, and he'd been about to drag her off our land when my uncle stepped in. He had beaten Boyle almost to death and then called his pack to come and get him before he was killed. Boyle's alpha at the time had sworn Boyle would never set foot out of wolf territory again.

Clearly, Price had no issues with reversing that order the second he became alpha.

The bear and wolf-shifters had a long history together. I was still amazed Price had become pack leader instead of Boyle. Price, I'd heard, had brains for business and money, and he'd

made the pack very wealthy over the past few decades, but he wasn't a trueborn leader. Boyle, on the other hand, had alpha blood running through his veins, yet he'd somehow become the subordinate, and Price had been allowed to take over. Either way, I hadn't cared too much. I didn't meddle in other packs' affairs—at least not until I had to, like now.

I watched Boyle sniffing around the base of the cliff. I knew they'd brought The Hunt here for a different reason. Price wasn't an idiot. If the police found bodies, it would be because Price wanted them to be found.

*So why bring The Hunt here? And why did he choose this particular woman?*

My claws dug deeper as I fought the urge to charge down there and take them on. I'd keep Boyle alive and beat the truth out of him, give him a matching scar on the other side of his face. It was tempting, so tempting. I could already feel my claws sinking through flesh like butter. Then I remembered the woman. She could get caught in the middle. If I went down there, I could be risking her life, and my bear huffed in protest at seeing her hurt.

So I stayed put and waited.

Boyle crept closer to where the crevice rested just feet above the wolf's shaggy head. I made a deep-throated pulsing sound low in my throat. Boyle started to raise his head, and then another wolf's howl echoed from farther off. With a snarl, Boyle turned away from the cliff and loped back into the trees with the other two wolves.

The woman would be safe for the night.

# CHAPTER 26

## RAVEN

I AWOKE, confused. I wasn't sure why I was so cold or why my limbs were so cramped. I cried out when I stretched my arms and attempted to get feeling back into my legs. They'd fallen asleep when I tightly curled up, trying to hide from the wolves and keep warm through the night. Once I disentangled myself from my ball, I scooted to the edge of the crevice and peered out.

The area seemed to be clear. I moved the brush out of the way, making an effort to avoid the snow falling off it, and began to climb down, but I slipped on some ice and plummeted a few feet with a muffled cry. Dazed from getting the wind knocked out of me, I stared up at the dark sky. It still looked like it might storm.

"Great. Just what I need."

I slowly got up from the deep snowdrift I'd landed in. At least it had cushioned my fall, but now I was cold. Maybe I should try starting a fire. No, it wouldn't be safe. I needed to get moving.

I stumbled along, struggling to get some warmth back into my legs and arms.

# CHAPTER 27

## BEAR

I smelled blood, and my bear snarled. It wasn't mine, and it wasn't from the other shifters. It was the woman. I'd know that scent anywhere.

I knew she was nearby, but other footsteps were approaching. Grant and Cutter had come to report their findings from the night. I shifted with a loud roar and walked to where I'd buried some supplies. We had many stashes like this all over our territory. Grant and Cutter shifted as well and then came to greet me.

"The wolves are all back at the campsite, but it looks like they're packing up," Cutter remarked.

"Fine. We'll just have to keep an eye on them and then draw them out more," I replied.

"Why not just take them now?" Grant asked, checking his Glock to make sure it was loaded. "It's daylight. We can see them. We know where they are, and we know they don't have the woman."

I growled, trying to hold in my temper. "Because we're trying *not* to start a war."

"Why bother trying?" Cutter asked. "They obviously want one."

"Do you want to explain a war to Taggert? Or why it'd be worse than anything he thinks he knows about? No, we stick to the plan. We draw them out. We get Price. We go home." I took a whiff of the wind and blew air out my nose. "Blood." A sharp pain pinged around in my head. "The woman's hurt," I hissed.

Grant and Cutter smirked at each other.

"Her name's Raven Holiday. That's what I heard the wolves calling her," Grant stated.

*Raven Holiday,* my beast repeated in reverence.

"You know," Cutter interjected, "she's pretty damn resilient for a human. She's not just some pathetic pushover."

My eye twitched. "And?"

"And we know you have this tough exterior..." Cutter went on. "But the clan would love for you to take a mate, any mate really."

My nostrils flared. "We're not discussing this again."

"Someone has to," Grant muttered under his breath.

I turned with a growl.

"Just pointing out the obvious. Your bear likes her. We can sense it as much as you can." He held his hands up in surrender when I took a menacing step toward him.

Grant backed away and tapped Cutter's arm. "Never mind. Let's go, Cutter, and keep an eye on Price and his pack."

The two of them stalked off through the trees, still mumbling about Raven being my mate.

"I can still hear you," I fumed.

Cutter turned and saluted me, and then he and Grant shifted and lumbered into the woods. Grant nearly disappeared, his white fur blending into the snowdrifts. Cutter stuck out until he was within the trees, and then his dark brown fur hid him well enough.

I sighed, watching them. I knew they wanted me to be happy, find a mate, and have a lot of cubs.

*But with a human?*

I wasn't even sure if the rest of the clan would accept that.

Over the years, mixed couples of bear shifters and witches or tigress shifters had been accepted within the clan, but never between an alpha and a human.

It didn't help that I'd never exactly been the relationship type. Too many times I'd tried to settle down with a bear, thinking all was well. Then Taggert would call me away on a secret mission, and I'd leave, not knowing when I'd be back or if I'd come back.

The women in my clan were strong, but apparently not strong enough. They'd all left me, arguing it was too emotionally draining not knowing if I'd return. But I knew the real reason they'd worried. If I decided to mate, claiming one, and I died, my mate would no longer be the alpha female of the clan. She could very well be killed in the struggle to find a new alpha.

Shifter life wasn't always easy, but it was far less brutal than it used to be. I tried to make my clan understand that. We no longer killed humans for fun and had an uneasy truce with most Protectors—a bloodline of humans who'd known about the existence of shifters for centuries. Protectors kept us in line by hunting and killing any feral and rogue shifters that harmed humans. I wondered if they knew what Price had been doing all these years or how many of those dead bodies were Protectors.

Maybe I should give Travis, the leader of the Protectors, a call and disrupt the wolves' plans. I was about to pull out my satellite phone when the wind blew angrily against my face. I caught the scent of blood again, and it was stronger this time.

Panic forced me to step forward, and before I knew what I was doing, I stripped, shifted, and was back on all fours, bones reshaping and snapping into place as the bear forced me forward.

It needed to find Raven, needed to see her.

There was the scent of blood, but no cries of triumph from the wolves. They weren't nearby at all.

*So how is she hurt?*

I loped forward, tearing up snow as I went. I had to know she was all right. I tried to fight my animal instincts to protect

her, but they were too strong. All I could do was hang on for the ride as my bear ran on, searching for her.

As I approached the stream, I found her leaning over the bank. The stream was mostly frozen over, but she'd managed to break through the thin layer of ice, and she was now drinking water.

Even from where I was, I could sense her fear, her intense pain. She shivered as the icy water went down her chin. I fought the urge to go to her and keep her warm as I kept to the shadows and observed.

Raven's hand froze halfway back to the water, and she whirled around. "Okay, you stalking motherfucker, I know you're out there."

I flinched. *Is she talking about me or Price?*

"Why are you watching me, huh? What do you want? You want to kill me, too?" she shrilled.

*Me?*

She was definitely talking about me.

Her voice had wavered and she'd sounded confused.

*Where is she hurt? Did she hit her head?*

I watched as she slowly stood and glanced around. She held her right leg a bit off the ground but didn't seem to realize she was doing it. For a few long seconds, she simply stared, her gaze roving across the tree line near the stream. Her eyes had lost a bit of the fire they'd had the first time I came face to face with her.

She was getting weaker.

Price and his pack would only grow more determined the longer she stayed away from them.

Raven was running out of time, which meant so was I. I needed to save her life to stop a war.

Suddenly, Raven's intense gaze zeroed in on my position. I froze. My heart pounded. Something warmed me, running through my veins, as I stared right back at her. She didn't even realize I was there.

Her presence alone was intoxicating, and I found myself slowly moving forward. All I could see was her in my arms, her kissing me, her wearing nothing but a sheet pooled at her waist with her pouty lips around my throbbing manhood.

My shaft thickened. I was within feet of the tree line when I forced myself to stop.

*What the hell am I thinking? Shit.*

There was no time for X-rated fantasies, and coming out of the trees like this would probably just scare the shit out of her.

Looking beaten down and tired, Raven turned back to the stream, took one last drink, and then headed on her way. She was still going south, and for the most part, she was staying close to water. She probably knew where the stream led. There was a small security post ten miles from where she was and, past that, the outskirts of a tiny town outside my territory. If she made it there, she'd be safe from the wolves—unless they were bold enough to try to take her out in the open. Then again, they'd brought The Hunt all the way up here.

Price knew this was my territory. Every shifter sensed where another's territory was.

*So why did he risk his pack members' lives by bringing it here?*

# CHAPTER 28

## GRANT

I LAY DOWN in the snowdrift, close to where the wolf pack had stopped to eat, and I listened to their conversations.

Mostly, they were talking about Raven and finding her before nightfall. They looked a bit nervous as they kept glancing at Price and flinching. Their alpha must have threatened them.

I would have to let Bear know things had escalated quickly. We'd only have until nightfall now to get Raven somewhere safe.

I focused on Price. He stepped away from the group with a satellite phone in hand. I needed to get closer to hear. Carefully, I crawled through the snow. It covered my scent for the most part, but then this entire area was covered in bear smells. It was our home, our territory, and the wolves were trespassing.

I stopped moving forward when I was able to pick up on what Price was saying. He kept clenching his left fist and gritting his teeth.

*Who could possibly anger him this much?*

"I understand, but we've had complications. Yes. Yes, I know. We're doing our best, but we followed tradition. We had to release her and hunt her down like the others. Of course I know that, you idiot." Price blanched and immediately stared down at his feet. "I'm sorry, sir. ... Yes, my temper. I apologize. We will

have the girl soon, and then you can do what you will with her. How are the other plans progressing?"

I listened intently to the rest of the conversation while part of my mind tried to get a grip on what I'd heard. This wasn't a normal *Hunt*. They weren't going to kill Raven here. *They're going to take her, but where?*

"The bears have been around, yes, but they're just watching. They act like they don't want to be the ones to start it, but don't worry. There will be a war. I can promise you that."

*Shit.*

So Price did want to start a war, which meant we would have to do everything we could to stop it.

We couldn't let Raven be killed or taken from our territory. And if we took out Price, we would have to do it quietly and kill the rest of them, too. This simple mission had just gotten a hell of a lot more complicated.

I waited until Price hung up before I slowly backed my way into the trees. Then I turned and ran to find Bear and alert him about Price's plan.

# CHAPTER 29

## RAVEN

My head felt fuzzy. I shivered in my coat as sweat dripped from my forehead. Something was wrong, but I was too exhausted to realize what it was.

My vision kept blurring, and as I stumbled through the snowdrifts, each step felt heavier than the last. I wasn't sure I was going to make it anymore.

Something large moved to my right, and I came to a shaky halt.

"I know you're there. I can see you," I hissed.

I had no idea what was out there, but acting like I did felt better than letting the thing continue to stalk me. It wasn't Price. If it were, he would've come out already to taunt me or kill me—or both. I knew when Price and his pack did finally catch me, my death wouldn't be swift. I'd be like that elk, eaten bit by bit as they watched me writhe in agony.

"Stop it," I scolded myself. "That's not helping. You have to stay positive and strong, remember? You want to get back home and find a man, someone who's not an asshole and who will love you. He'll overlook the fact that you don't know shit about being normal, and he'll be hung like a fucking horse because you haven't been fucked in months." I continued to mutter to myself.

Then I laughed when I realized I sounded like a raving lunatic.

*Shit. Maybe I am crazy.*

*How could I not go a little insane after everything I've seen?*

"I'm not crazy. I'm just tired and fucking starving," I added when my stomach growled. I stopped and took a deep breath to steady myself, but all it did was give my stomach a chance to growl even louder. "I get it. You're hungry. Well, that's just too fucking bad. Deal with it."

But damn... what I wouldn't give for a big, sloppy hamburger with a large side of cheese fries and a shake.

I started on again, one heavy step at a time, determined to make good distance today. I knew somewhere along this stream was a ranger station. If I could just get there, I'd make it. I'd survive this nightmare.

*Unless the other thing stalking me decides to eat me first.*

I stopped again and turned around really quick, hoping to catch it, but there were only trees. I bent down, and laughing hysterically, I started to make a snowball. Part of my brain told me I was being a complete idiot. The other part of my brain told that part to shut the fuck up.

I picked up the well-formed snowball and chucked it into the trees.

"Boo-yah!" I danced halfheartedly, twerking as if I were in a club. "Take that, you fucker." I bent down, made another snowball that I had to hold with both hands, and launched it. "You sure you want to rumble with me?"

But then this one hit something solid, and it wasn't a tree. There was a low animal-like sound.

*Oh, shit!*

I froze as a shadow separated itself from the trees and lumbered forward, pieces of my snowball falling from its wide shoulders.

"Oh, hell no!" I screamed as the grizzly stalked hungrily toward me.

My eyes darted around, but there was nowhere to run. Anyway, I couldn't outrun it; that was for damn sure. It was going to eat me. Well, at least that would be better than being caught by Price—though how, I wasn't sure yet.

The bear stalked closer, sniffing the air. It was beautiful, but at the same time, it was deadly. Gawking at it, it was larger than any grizzly I'd ever seen. Its head was easily the size of my torso. Its paws were bigger than my head, and it was tall, even on all fours.

This wasn't just a grizzly. It was a monster.

It shifted ever so slightly as it came toward my trembling body, and I caught sight of the familiar marks on its back. I had no doubt this was the same bear from my dreams. For just a second, I forgot to be terrified that something else had just come out of the woods to eat me.

*Dammit. I fucking pissed it off.*

The markings definitely didn't look natural, but they didn't seem out of place either. The lines of color weren't straight, but wavy, almost forming an intricate tribal-looking design. I wasn't sure what it was supposed to be, but I couldn't stop staring at them. Even when the grizzly was only feet from me and I could feel its hot breath on my face, all I saw were those markings.

Then the bear roared, and I was right back to being scared.

Its eyes weren't normal for a bear either. Sky blue, they bored right into my very soul, and I was frozen. The bear took another step toward me, and something snapped inside my head. I was hungry, exhausted, and tired of feeling out of control. Helpless and scared, I was going to die out here at the hands of beasts.

The fear started to ebb as my anger grew. I refused to move away from the bear. I didn't back away from anything.

My fists clenched and unclenched at my sides. There was no way in hell I was going to let a bear—or anything else for that matter—kill me. If this were a shifter, I sure as hell wasn't going to go down easy.

I reacted swiftly. Rearing my arm back, I smacked the bear on the muzzle. "Get the hell away from me, asshole."

The bear glared back at me, eyes wide before they narrowed, and a guttural growl started in its chest.

I grunted back. "Oh, go ahead. Snarl at me," I snapped, pointing in its face while wagging my hand. "I don't give a shit. In fact, all of you fucking monsters can kiss my freezing ass." I turned around, bent forward, and nearly toppled over before slapping my ass. "Go ahead. Kiss it," I demanded, looking over my shoulder.

The bear didn't move. It continued to eyeball me as its grumble quieted.

"Just like I thought. You got nothing but a roar and no bite, just like in all my dreams." Turning back around to fully face the bear, I jammed my hands on my hips. "Well, this time I'm not helpless and stuck in some fucking icy hole, begging for my life, while you get ready to attack me. Nope, this time I'm free to punch you in the damn throat and send your big ass running." I shook my fist at it. "Run along now before I get to beating your ass like you owe me money."

I waited for it to rip me into pieces, but instead, it just glared at me. A wave of dizziness hit me, and I swayed, barely staying on my feet. I needed help, badly, and standing here arguing with a bear was crazy.

"Fine, then. If you're not going to go away, I will," I said, still trying to sound tougher than I felt. "Watch my ass go right on through the woods, grizzly."

Everything was getting topsy-turvy. I stumbled away from the bear, trying to ignore the fact that I'd just smacked a bear in the face and told it to kiss my ass.

*What the hell was I thinking?*

I hurried through the snow, glancing over my shoulder every few minutes to check the bear's proximity. Of course, there the bear was, lumbering after me. It kept its distance, and laughter bubbled up in my throat. It was probably scared of getting

smacked again. I kept laughing and continued to go along as if I didn't have a care in the world, as if a giant grizzly and a pack of wolves weren't trying to kill me.

*Yep, just another ordinary day for me. Nothing out of sorts here. Nope. I'll just keep on trekking.*

# CHAPTER 30

## BEAR

I WAS STILL in shock as I followed Raven, almost as if I were in a trance. She'd smacked me, just reached up and fucking smacked the shit out of me.

*A grizzly bear. In the face with her bare hand.*

I watched her luscious ass—the ass she'd slapped like a stripper and told me to kiss—as it jiggled slightly while she trudged on.

*Who the hell is this woman?*

She whirled around, sticking up her middle finger at me. "Go away, asshole," she snarled, swaying on her feet before turning back around and slowly walking off.

She was going to pass out. I'd smelled the blood on her, but there was an infection, too. She had a fever, and it was making her delirious. I wasn't sure just how bad she was until Grant came stalking out of the woods, and Raven spotted him.

Waiting to see what she'd do, I watched Grant freeze in place.

*Should I go?* Grant asked.

I shook my furry head. *No, she doesn't think this is real. Just don't move.*

Grant yawned loudly, then plopped his bear butt in the snow

and waited. Raven stared at him for a few seconds, and then she glanced back over her shoulder at me before looking back at him.

"You're a polar bear," she mused. "Why the fuck are you here? Oh, damn. This isn't right. This isn't real. It can't be."

The thought must have made her happy because she laughed, and then she reached out a hand toward Grant's muzzle. He didn't move an inch. She looked so small compared to his body.

Raven's fingers brushed his muzzle, and he nuzzled against her hand. Then he blew out through his nose loudly before sneezing. A pang of jealousy shot through me at the sight, and I growled.

Grant quirked a brow at me. *Don't like her, huh?* he joked. *I'll take her.*

*Enough,* I answered through our link.

But I couldn't deny it any longer. Raven had pulled me to her somehow, making me feel like it would be the death of me if I ever left her side.

But now it seemed if we left her, she would die.

Raven started to move on past Grant, as if she were used to seeing polar bears in the middle of the Canadian wild. She hit a few more yards before I recognized something was amiss. She stumbled forward and began to go down. Grant ran to her, and she landed on his hulk of a body, unconscious. I rushed over, shifting back to my human form, and pulled her upward into my arms.

Grant shifted moments later. "She has an infection. I can smell it."

"I know. We have to get the wound patched up, but I don't want her knowing we helped—not yet."

"So she's going to wake up in an altogether new spot with a bandaged wound?"

"Yes. She's already been through enough. I'm not dying to make her face the truth that more than wolf-shifters are out here. I have a feeling she doesn't think I'm really a bear." I began

to turn away when Grant reached out a hand and rested it on my shoulder. "What?"

"I need to tell you something before you decide on what to do."

"Spit it out. We don't have time."

"That's precisely what I'm attempting to tell you. They're going to come after her with everything they have tonight, but not to kill her."

I swallowed hard, still angry and not sure about what was going on.

Grant continued. "They're going to take her back to their territory."

"That doesn't make any fucking sense."

"It sounded like someone was waiting for her there. Price never revealed a name."

I pulled Raven closer to my bare chest, wanting to protect her. We could bandage her up, but if we left her alone again in the wild, Price and the others would find her.

"So this isn't about The Hunt. It's a kidnapping."

Grant nodded silently. "But I'm not sure why they chose her."

No way was I going to let her out of my sight now. Raven was going to have to stay with us whether she wished it or not. Maybe she wouldn't have to know she was being watched so closely. I had a feeling she wasn't the type to take help lightly. And being in the presence of more supernatural beings was likely going to have the opposite effect of what I wanted when we would officially meet.

"We'll get her patched up the best we can, and then maybe we can try to use their attack tonight to trap them. But we cannot kill them, if at all possible," I added. "Make sure Cutter understands that when you get to him." As I moved around, Raven still tucked safely in my arms, I mumbled, "Cutter's reckless mind gets in front of him."

"Just like your heart's getting ahead of you?"

I stopped and turned with a glower. "What did you say?"

"It's obvious you want her, Bear. If you have no feelings for the woman, use her as bait to draw out Price and then bargain with him."

"Have you grown that fucking cold over the years? To use an innocent human like that?"

"No, but the alpha I know would have never thought twice about using a human as bait."

"She could die."

"Or she could lead us right to Price and whatever else is going on. Then we can end this before it starts."

I wanted to argue, but Grant was right. Normally, using a human to get what we needed never would have been a question. I didn't hate non-shifters, but I didn't feel a connection to them either.

*So why not use Raven? She's just a human, just a normal everyday human that should mean nothing at all to me.*

There was absolutely no reason I shouldn't use her. The chances of her actually getting hurt were slim. If everything went well enough, she'd just be used to flush Price and his plans out into the open.

The second I started to seriously consider it, my bear revolted, snarling and growling loud enough to make my head hurt. I staggered, trying to remain upright, as the bear went on and on. I was forced to stand completely still so I wouldn't fall with Raven in my arms.

"No," I finally managed to snap. "I will not use her as bait."

"We could stop a war, Bear. That's a bit more important than just one human life, isn't it?"

I wanted to say yes, but my bear wouldn't let me. No other life was more important than Raven's. "We'll take her back to camp and figure out what to do from there. Get Cutter."

"If you say so, Alpha," Grant returned.

I snarled under my breath, but Grant was already heading back into the trees to find Cutter. I wasn't sure what had gotten

into the shifter, but I wasn't about to use Raven as any sort of lure. I'd been content to let Price and his pack try to hunt her down, but to actually set a trap and use her... That shit was out of the question.

I wasn't going to do that, not ever.

I had a fucking suspicion this insane woman, who had smacked a grizzly bear, was never going to leave my sight again.

# CHAPTER 31

## GRANT

I CAUGHT up to Cutter as he observed the wolves from atop a ridge. We were upwind, so the wolves couldn't smell us, not that they would be able to tell the difference from the old scent and where they were now. They were too focused on finding their next campsite.

They were in human form. It would be so easy to catch them off guard and take them out now.

But I had my orders.

"What's the news?" Cutter asked while I shifted back to human form.

Grabbing my set of clothes, I got dressed. "Bear wants us back at camp. He has Raven."

"He has her? I thought we were staying out of her affairs."

"We were, but she has a fever and an infection somewhere. She wouldn't last another night on her own, so he's taken it upon himself to rescue her."

Something in my tone made Cutter laugh. "Is it like we thought?"

"I believe so. Our alpha has finally found a possible mate, no matter how much he's fighting it." I grinned as Cutter laughed quietly.

For years, we'd been hoping to find the right woman for Bear. He'd been set up with every single woman we could find, and now, it took us being in the woods, hunting down one of the most dangerous wolf-shifter packs, for him to find her. It was a bit unusual that she was a human, but shifter-human couples weren't anything new. It was just uncommon for her to be the alpha's mate.

Cutter continued. "Then I guess we'd better get back to camp. I need to check in at home again and make sure Kyle isn't bringing down the house."

"Or starting a war of his own," I growled.

We backed into the shadows of the trees. The sky had darkened once more. More storms were on the way. I could smell it in the breeze every time it blew.

I had to catch Cutter up on what I'd heard, too. I was still baffled as to why the wolf-shifters would kidnap Raven and who wanted her so badly.

As far as I knew, the woman was nothing special. We'd already run a check on her, just to see if she had any connection whatsoever to the wolves. But not a thing out of the ordinary had come up. She was a woman who'd been abandoned as a baby. There was zilch interesting until she'd gone to college, graduated, and taken her current job, escorting the wealthy on adventure trips.

But most women I knew, humans or shifters, didn't have that fire I'd seen in her eyes. With her determination to keep going, to live, she had a very strong will, and I was curious to see if Bear would realize she was his true match.

# CHAPTER 32

## RAVEN

I WAS MOVING, but I wasn't sure how. I felt warm, like I was floating in air. Somewhere, I must have passed out, but the last thing I remembered was falling out of the crevice.

*How long has it been?*

*What if I'm not alone?*

I screamed as I thought of being captured by Price. I fought against whatever was holding me, breaking away from its warmth.

I wanted to be let go.

I wasn't going to be eaten alive. It would not happen. I'd die first. I screamed and punched, trying to get away, but I quickly exhausted myself.

A gentle touch brushed against my forehead, soothing me. I relaxed slowly and opened my eyes, only to see shadows around me.

*People.*

*Have I been rescued finally?*

"You're going to be all right," a rough, masculine voice declared. "Lie back and try to relax."

"Wolves... they were shifters," I whispered.

"Just relax now and sleep," the voice implored.

It was deep, guttural, and it touched something hidden within me, sending delicious shivers down my back. I nodded, and as the hand smoothed back my hair, I relaxed, letting the darkness overtake me again.

# CHAPTER 33

## BEAR

I RAN my hand through Raven's hair, loving the feel of it through my fingers. It was a beautiful shade of brown with streaks of lighter cinnamon and dark strands of black running through it. Her hazel eyes were mesmerizing, but they were closed again, which was probably a good thing. When she woke up, I knew it was going to be difficult to explain to her that my team and I were not like the wolf-shifters. But I'd worry about that when the time came.

We'd needed to take her coat off, so I rubbed my hands against her bare arms to keep her warm. Cutter built up the fire as Grant took a look at Raven's leg. We'd found the cut after I sniffed it out. It wasn't very long, but it was a deep puncture mark. She'd probably fallen on a rock and never felt a thing.

"It won't need stitches," Grant said as he examined it, "but I will have to clean out the infection. It's going to hurt."

I held Raven's shoulders down the best I could without hurting her and nodded. Grant told Cutter to stand by with the homemade salve Aunt Kristine had concocted and stowed in my bag with fresh bandages and tape. The second the pus was pushed out, he'd need to clean it and then quickly bandage it.

Grant took Raven's hurt leg and, pressing his fingers against

either side of the wound, he started to squeeze and push. Raven stirred a bit but didn't wake up. Grant squeezed harder, and the cloudy white liquid oozed from the opening in her skin.

She groaned in pain and shifted, but I whispered soothing words in her ear, keeping her as calm as I could. A few minutes later, the wound was cleared out and cleaned before Grant finished bandaging it.

"Her fever should break soon enough," he told me. "She needs some water and food, though."

I nodded, distracted, as I continued to stroke my fingers down Raven's cheek.

Grant nudged Cutter. "We're going to keep a lookout while you wake her up and get her to eat something." They stormed away.

Once they were out of sight, I took a deep breath and then gently tapped Raven's cheeks before shaking her until her eyes opened.

"Wake up. Come on. Up and at 'em, Raven."

Her eyes twitched and she groaned, trying to move. It took a few minutes, but she finally opened her eyes. I smiled, but her eyes darted around in alarm, and she struggled to get away from me.

"Your eyes. You're that grizzly bear... a bloodthirsty shifter. Get away from me."

I raised my arms and backed away. "Raven, you're safe here. I promise. I'm not like Price and his pack."

"I don't fucking believe you." She fought to move to her feet. "Ouch." She staggered. "What did you do to me?"

"We patched you up," I told her, still sitting by the fire. "You had a puncture wound and an infection, so we took care of it. Your fever should go down as soon as we can get you to eat and drink something." I held out a thermos with steaming chicken broth and a small bag of jerky. "Please, eat something."

Raven shook her head and started to walk away, but she swayed and nearly fell. I lunged forward and caught her. She

fought her way out of my arms, and I let her go once she was back on the ground by the fire.

"How do I know I can trust you?" she snapped. "You're a shifter... thing."

"My name is Bear Armstrong, and currently, you're in bear-shifter territory—to be exact, *my* territory."

Raven's face froze before she broke out in laughter. "Bear-shifters, wolf-shifters... This is fucking unbelievable."

"This is not a fucking joke, Raven Holiday."

Her brow wrinkled. "How do you know my name?"

"From Price and his pack, but we confirmed it with my contact." I paused. "I work for a top-secret branch of the government," I informed her.

"Wait, so the government knows you exist? All of you?" Her voice squeaked.

"You'd be surprised what they actually know," I whispered, poking the fire with a stick.

"That still doesn't explain how you know about me," she accused.

"You were traveling with one of our targets. We had to know who you were, if and how you were affiliated with Price's pack."

Raven glared at me. "Do I look like a fucking wolf?"

"No, but I had to be sure you weren't working with him."

"Fine, whatever. I'm out of here." She got to her feet and started making her way, slowly and painfully moving away from me and the campfire.

*This woman is just plain stubborn.*

"Where are you going?"

"I've had enough of shifters and wolves and bears, oh my, to last me a damn lifetime. I'm getting my ass home."

"And you're going to do it on your own?"

She glanced back over her shoulder. "How else would I do it?"

"Fine, leave, but you haven't made it this far on your own," I

growled, growing more agitated by the second. *All I'm trying to do is help. Why does she have to be so damn stubborn?*

Raven stopped and turned all the way around to stare at me. "What do you mean? I haven't been eaten yet, have I?" She jammed her hands on her luscious hips.

I shifted my gaze up to her face, trying to steer my mind away from the sudden urge to body-slam her onto the ground and fuck her into submission. "Who do you think saved you the first night you ran off?"

She shook her head. "I wound up in a cave. That's what saved me, asshole."

I sighed heavily. "Do you remember how you got to that cave, darling?"

She started to nod, and then she stopped when she realized... she had no idea. Her eyes locked on mine.

"I don't need your help, Bear."

"Yes, you do, Raven. Now sit down and let yourself rest."

"No," she snapped. Then she turned and began to walk off again.

"I hauled you into that cave," I called out. "And last night, Price and his pack would've caught you had I not destroyed your campfire, covered up your tracks, and made sure my bear scent—instead of yours—was all over that cliff." I stood when she stopped walking again. "You can't do this alone, Raven. Let me help you."

She turned around and stared at me. "Why are you protecting me? Why would the fucking government care if I lived or died?"

I walked toward her until we were barely a foot apart. I was drawn to her, and the bear in me cried out for a connection, to feel her skin beneath my fingers, but I resisted. "They don't, but I do. You walked right into the middle of something that is far greater than just a hunt."

Her brow furrowed as she swayed on her feet. I knew she

really needed to sit back down, but I didn't want to tell her that. She was too strong-willed.

"Price told me they wanted to kill me."

"He lied."

I could tell there was a fight going on in her mind. Part of her wanted to stay, but part of her felt it would be weak to give in. She took one step backward and then another. When she started to turn away, I reached out and grabbed her arm.

She stopped. "Let me go."

I didn't want to. I wanted to pull her close in my arms and keep her there, but I let go anyway. And in that second, I saw the mark on her forearm.

"What is that?" I asked, pointing to it.

She shrugged. "A birthmark. Why?" She suspiciously looked at me.

"You were an orphan, right?"

Her eyes narrowed, and she yanked her arm back. "Why?"

"Raven... do you have any idea who your family was?"

She shook her head and threw her arms up in the air. "That's it. I'm done. Leave me alone. I've had it with wolves and bears and whatever else is out there!" she screamed. "I know where I'm going, so just leave me the hell alone." She rubbed her hands along her arms. "And give me my damn coat before I really get pissed and punch you in the throat."

I walked back over to the fire, got it, strode to her, and handed it to her. "Raven, Price won't stop until they have you," I said, trying to reason with her.

"Yeah, well, I'd like to see him try, because this chick isn't going down easy. Now leave me the fuck alone."

I should have just tied her down. Then I wouldn't have to worry about her, but I knew she'd hate me for it. I let her walk off, grumbling under her breath about shifters, wolves, bears, and who knew what else.

Cutter and Grant came back to my side a few moments later.

"That went well," Cutter mused after he whistled. "I'm assuming you still want us to follow her."

"Yes. I have a feeling she thinks she's dreaming this right now," I answered. "And Price will try to come for her tonight."

"Something else bothering you?" Grant asked.

"There's a mark on her arm. She was born with it."

Cutter and Grant glanced at each other before the latter whispered, "The mark of a Protector?"

"Looked like it. At least now we might know why Price wants her alive."

"Well, let's make sure we keep her that way." Cutter slapped me on the back. "Wouldn't want anything to happen to our alpha's mate, would we?"

Grant cursed under his breath.

I turned and glared at Cutter. "My what?"

"Never mind. Let's go," Cutter told Grant with a wide grin before heading after Raven.

"Damn fuckers," I mumbled, standing there rooted to the spot.

Was it that obvious—what I felt for Raven? If she were my mate, I would have a hell of a fight coming my way, trying to convince her she belonged to me.

She didn't even trust me right now, not that I could really blame her. I'd seen that look before on many humans' faces. If they saw something like a shifter, their brains would just refuse to believe it was real. It was too far outside the norm. She wouldn't believe it until she had nothing left to doubt.

Either way, it left me in a delicate position. Price would be coming after her tonight. We somehow needed to stop him without letting Raven get hurt.

"Looks like she's going to be bait after all," I whispered. My bear clacked his teeth in protest. "I tried, dammit. Now shut the fuck up." He slapped against my insides in retaliation. "You little fucker." I winced in pain. "The only thing that will stop her is if I

hogtied her." My bear grunted and stomped with approval. "Fuck no, I'm not tying her ass up."

Even though it did sound very tempting. A vision of the dark beauty tied to my king-size bed, butt naked, with my tongue in her glistening slit flashed through my head before I shook it away.

No, Raven was going to do what she wanted. She hadn't needed anyone her whole life. She wasn't about to start now.

# CHAPTER 34

## RAVEN

"Bear. A fucking bear who's actually named Bear," I angrily babbled under my breath as I stumbled through the snow.

There was no damn denying that he was gorgeous and ripped. I couldn't get the vision of the way his T-shirt had clung to his broad shoulders and his wicked defined upper body. Primal lust gripped me with such intensity it almost hurt.

*Shit.* Under different circumstances, I would have climbed Bear's ass like a fucking tree and dry-humped him into submission.

*Dammit. Why did he have to be just my type?*

Hot with short, silky jet-black hair, a sensual mouth, and a set of piercing sky-blue eyes that made me want to rip his damn clothes off and have my freaky, dirty way with him.

"Stupid shifters," I grumbled. "Why should I trust him? Just because he says he helped me? Or because he appeared in my dreams?" I pushed a branch out of the way. It whipped forward, almost smacking me in the face. "He shoved me in a damn cave. If he really wanted to help me, he would've just gotten me out of here, right? Bastard Bear."

There was no reason for me to trust him. Even if I wanted to

turn right back around and let him curl his huge body around me so I could feel his warmth, hear his rough voice—

*Nope. Not happening.*

I couldn't be sure if he was trying to help me or kill me. Maybe he just wanted to use me. I had nothing to gain by trusting him. I'd find my way back to the stream and make it to the ranger station.

They'd save me. Humans—normal, everyday humans—would get me home, and maybe this time, I wouldn't feel the need to leave again. Maybe I'd even quit the agency and just travel the world until I found somewhere that felt like home.

Self-consciously, I scratched at my arm, the one with the birthmark. When I was a kid, I used to get made fun of because of it, and I'd normally cover it up. No one had seen it, not even Halle, in years.

Then Bear did.

I felt the need to stare at it. I stopped walking and slowly pushed up my coat sleeve. I ran my index finger over the mark. It was pale, a stark contrast against my dark skin. For the longest time, the actual shape of the mark had eluded me.

But now, after spending so much time around weird things—

My jaw dropped when I realized what it looked like—a paw print with something going through the middle.

*A knife maybe?*

"What the hell?" I eyed it for a long time before I heard rustling behind me.

When I turned, no one was there, but I had a feeling Bear wasn't going to let me go as easily as I'd hoped.

*Or is it Price and the others?*

That thought got me hurrying, and I started to run as fast as I could with my injured leg, blocking out the pain.

*I'll get somewhere safe, away from all this shit, and never look at that mark on my arm again.*

# CHAPTER 35

## BEAR

I HADN'T SEEN a mark like the one on Raven's arm in person, but I had on one of the pages of my clan's history books. It was rare and was associated with the Protectors. And from the look on Raven's face, she had no idea what it meant.

I was running out of time. I didn't want Taggert to know more than he needed to, but right now, I didn't have a choice.

I called the base and asked for him. "Tell him it's Armstrong and it's urgent."

"Right away, sir."

I paced around the fire as more snow started to fall around me. I kicked at the drifts until Taggert finally picked up the line.

"Armstrong, you'd better have good news for me."

"Sir, did something change on your end?"

"We have massive movement at Price's main residence and on his land. The body count is still rising," Taggert declared. "I want this monster brought in and soon."

"I understand that, but, sir, we have a bit of a complication."

I caught Taggert up on the difficulties of the situation. I contemplated leaving out the details of The Hunt, but with the number of bodies Taggert's men had been turning up, the man

needed to know everything. The conversation was mostly one-sided as I told him the laws of The Hunt, how it had been outlawed long ago, and how Price and his pack were obviously still practicing it.

"They brought Raven up here to hunt her, but it might be more complex than that."

"But she doesn't know why they picked her?" Taggert asked.

"No. I need you to do something for me, sir."

"Right now, if it'll bring this bastard in, I'll do whatever you need, Armstrong."

"Raven Holiday is an orphan. I need you to dig up any information you can on who her parents might have been."

Taggert relayed the information to a tech. "I'll get back to you as fast as I can, Armstrong. Are you sure she's not involved?"

"She's not helping them. She's definitely a victim here. I just need to know why."

"All right. I'll be in touch. Stay safe, Armstrong, and later, you'll fill me in on this Hunt business."

I hung up, hoping I wouldn't regret telling Taggert all of that. But I needed information on Raven, needed to know who she was. If she were the daughter of Protectors, why did they give her up at birth? Usually, they'd raise their children in the family business. I'd never heard of Protectors giving up their children. But it might have something to do with whoever was awaiting Raven back at Price's home.

*An old grudge maybe?* Maybe Raven's parents had killed a prominent member of the pack, and Raven was their way of exacting revenge.

And Price had brought her all the way up here to try to provoke me into starting a war, which meant Price wasn't about to give up easily.

Raven was in trouble. Price might not wait until nightfall to attack. And I'd let her wander off into the wilderness with only two bears to protect her against a group of seven ferocious wolves.

I cursed and then took off into the trees, racing to find Raven and the others, hoping I wasn't too late to warn them about Price's plan.

# CHAPTER 36

## RAVEN

I HAD STOPPED RUNNING when the snow started falling again. It was going to get colder and colder, and the snow was just going to keep coming down. There was no use in depleting all my energy now. I didn't sense anything wrong, so I figured a slow, steady pace would get me where I needed to go well enough.

The path I took led into a small valley. For a second, I wondered if I should go around. The hair on the back of my neck stood on end, and I felt my gut clench.

Something wasn't right.

The sun was still up, but the valley was dark, and the storm rolling in was only starting to make it worse. If I went in there, I wouldn't be able to see very well. I rubbed the spot on my arm again and started to turn back, when something growled loudly behind me.

My blood ran cold. I turned slowly in the snow, trying to keep my balance.

Three wolves, heads easily reaching my shoulders, stood a good distance behind me. They snarled and flashed their large white canines at me. Spittle dripped from their mouths, and as one force, they unhurriedly started making their way through the snow toward me.

I had no weapons, nothing to fight them off with.

*Dammit, I should have stayed with the big, bad sexy Bear.*

I walked backward, one step at a time, with my eyes glued on the wolves.

*Why aren't they attacking?*

I should have been on my back by now, fighting them off and screaming for my life.

But they were waiting.

*Why?*

My foot rolled onto something under the snow, and I noticed the large stick. Calmly, I bent down and picked it up, holding it like a bat.

"I'll beat the shit out of you, assholes, if you come one step closer," I threatened. "Get back. You hear me? Get away from me."

They stepped closer. I swung at them, but they easily stayed out of my reach. I was too hungry, tired, and weak. The stick was heavier than it should have been in my grip.

*Shit, when was the last time I'd eaten anything?*

My leg throbbed, and I tried not to put weight on it, but then I was off balance. Another wild swing caused me to fall on my side. "Dammit."

The stick rolled away, and when I reached out a hand to grab it, one of the wolves snapped its jaws and leapt for it first, planting its front paws firmly on it.

I pulled my hand back. My heart raced and my breathing was ragged. I wasn't going to cry from frustration, not now. I wasn't going to give them the satisfaction. If I were going to die, I'd die while somehow taking one of them out with me.

And I'd die without screaming or begging.

Hands going numb from the snow, I tried to crawl my way backward. The wolves only moved in closer and closer. I could feel their hot breaths on my skin, smell the blood of whatever they'd just killed. It made me gag.

The wolves stopped. Their ears twitched. The one in the

middle tilted its head and turned, almost looking confused. I wasn't sure what was going on until I saw the giant shape of a bear lumbering toward us, full speed.

*A polar bear?*

The bear rammed into the three wolves and sent them scattering just as another grizzly, smaller than the one I remembered, with no special markings, ran up next to me. The logical part of my mind screamed for me to run, but there was something about the eyes. This bear wasn't going to hurt me. It stood protectively in front of me and snarled as the polar bear closed in, and the three wolves charged back.

The white bear roared and swatted the first wolf away with its paw, but the other two lunged for its back. I watched behind the grizzly as the wolves scratched and bit the other bear. The grizzly reared back on its hind legs, large feet just inches from crushing me, before it charged forward and went to pull the wolves off its comrade.

I scooted back in the snow and kept going until I heard another growl right behind me. Something large breathed down my neck, and I froze.

Paws appeared on either side of me, and when I tilted my head back, I was staring into the scarred black muzzle of Boyle. The scar he had as a human was even more terrifying on his wolf face.

The black wolf raised a lip, flashing bloodstained canines. I tried to move away, but I wasn't fast enough. Boyle's jaws opened, and he bit down on my shoulder. I screamed as I felt his teeth tearing through flesh and into the bone. Hot tears pricked my eyes as I punched Boyle's face, trying to make him let go, but all he did was bite down harder. Blood warmed my arm as it trailed down my shoulder. The pain was immense, and my vision started to blur. He dragged me backward, and I knew this was it. This was going to be the end.

The ground shook beneath my body, and whining filled my

ears. Several of the wolves scattered. I tried to see what was happening, tried to focus.

A third bear appeared behind the first two, twice their size. This was Bear. The markings on his back were as plain as day, even with the snow falling heavier and heavier. The bear's lips were pulled back in an ugly snarl. It opened its mouth, stood up on its hind legs, and roared so loud it hurt my ears. Boyle instantly released me and jumped in front of me, but the bear wasn't having any of it.

It roared again and fell back on all fours, ready to charge forward, when a distant howl made Boyle's ears flinch backward. He looked like he still wanted to attack the bear, but the howl sounded again, louder, closer. Boyle howled briefly back, growled at the others, and then took off back into the valley.

I forced myself to stay conscious a little longer, even as my blood dripped through my torn coat and into the snow. I was cold, and it was only getting worse.

I stared at the large grizzly and then watched in awe as it transformed from an animal back to a very naked Bear.

Even through the pain, all I could think was, *Damn. My other weakness—a man with a huge cock.*

He was tall—well over six feet if I had to guess. His skin was tan everywhere. He was definitely an outdoors man. An air of authority radiated from him, and it turned me on even more.

"Raven, can you hear me?" He hurried toward me, not caring about his nakedness. "Raven?"

His penetrating blue eyes locked on mine with an intense attention.

"You told the truth," I stated.

"I would never lie to you, darling." He smirked, but it didn't erase the worry in his eyes. "Just hang on. We'll get you back to camp."

I barely had the strength to nod before I felt him scooping me up into his arms.

Then I passed out.

# CHAPTER 37

## RAVEN

I WAS IN PAIN, lots of it. I felt tugging at my shoulder and winced. The wince turned into a groan as I tried to move away from the throbbing. Hands held me down as something sharp stabbed into me, and I nearly shot off the ground.

"Easy, Raven, we're just stitching up the wound."

I knew that voice. I loved that voice. *Bear*. I focused only on it while my shoulder was being stitched up. The pain was still present, but it was lessened by his voice.

Finally, it was over.

"Take a deep breath, darling," Bear commanded.

I opened my eyes and glanced up to see another gorgeous man, with stark-white hair and caramel skin, bandaging my shoulder. A third, a burly, rugged guy with tousled dark curls, paced nearby, tossing a knife up and down as he watched the surrounding trees.

I reached up for Bear's hand, still resting on my shoulder. "Thank you... all of you," I whispered.

The man bandaging me smirked as the other stopped his pacing and winked. "Sweetness, a kiss from you would be reward enough." He gave me a clown-wide smile.

I laughed. "Nice try, but that shit ain't happening."

Bear growled at him.

The clown-wide smiler held up his hands. "Come on, bro. I can't help myself. She's fucking gorgeous."

I winked at him. "You're not so bad yourself."

I wasn't kidding. With his sheer hotness and a set of piercing green eyes, he looked like he'd just walked off a fashion shoot. Still, I preferred the dark, broody, delicious Bear.

He made loud kissing sounds as he puckered his gorgeous chiseled lips.

My lips curled up at the edges. "But it's still a hard pass on the kiss, clown boy."

"You don't know what you're missing. I've been told by the ladies that my kisses curl toes."

I rolled my eyes. "I bet they do."

He laughed while stalking away from us, heading toward the forest.

"Don't mind him. He's not much older than a cub," Bear snapped.

"Heard that!" he shouted before disappearing into the thicket.

I smiled, already relaxing from the funny banter. "Who are you people?"

"The man patching you up is Grant, and the loudmouth is Cutter," Bear told me. "They were watching you when you were attacked, and they're the other part of my special ops team."

"Thank God for that," I whispered. "So, um... I guess you get to say I told you so." It was totally an ass move to stomp away from him like that when he'd only been trying to protect me.

"Why would I do that?" Bear asked.

Grant wiped a harsh-smelling liquid across the stitches. "You can move her now."

Bear carefully propped me up before wrapping an arm around my waist, and then he scooted me onto his lap as he moved to sit on the log.

I stiffened slightly and then relaxed. His lap was way more

comfortable than sitting on a hard log. Besides, his warm body pressed against my back and legs loosened the stiffness in my muscles.

"Well, I'm sorry for throwing that unbecoming tantrum and walking off. That shit wasn't cool." I reached over to hold my shoulder, staring at it for a long second before it dawned on me that I'd been bitten by a wolf-shifter. "Oh, shit!" My fingers trembled. "On the next full moon, I'm going to turn into a wolf, aren't I?"

A scene from a cheesy D-rated horror flick flashed through my mind. I was foaming at the mouth, running around in circles and ripping off my clothes while simultaneously morphing into a grotesque monster before howling at the moon... horribly off-key.

"What?" Bear asked.

I inched sideways on his lap and glared at him. "You know what the hell I'm talking about. Give it to me straight. Rip it off like a fucking Band-Aid. Will I turn into a wolf?"

"No, it doesn't work like that."

I could tell by the light in his eyes that he was trying not to laugh.

"You sure?" I squeaked. "Because I own a very nice condo in SoHo, and I can't be shifting in the middle of the night and racing through my building, attacking and eating my neighbors." My eyes narrowed. "Though there is that snotty blonde down the hall I've been itching to tear into pieces for walking her dog and not picking up his shit."

He laughed. The husky sound made me giddy, almost sending me to an ungraceful splat onto the ground.

Bear snaked his huge arm around me, firmly pinning me to him. "Yes, I'm sure. You're either born a shifter, or you're not. Trust me, Raven. You're safe."

Tilting my head back, I stared at him. "Okay. But if you're lying, I'm finding your ass and ripping out a huge chunk."

He smiled. "Do your worst. I'm not scared."

I smiled back. I shook away the vision of me licking and nipping my way up his muscular body. *Jesus, Raven, get your mind out of the gutter.* "Well, you should be. I'm hell on wheels when I'm pissed the fuck off."

He moved forward. Our faces were mere inches apart.

"Why aren't you afraid of me?" He stared at me with a mixed look of fascination and confusion. "Most humans would be curled up into a ball, screaming for their lives. But you're taking all of this in remarkable stride."

I shrugged and then winced from the pinch of my stitches. "Believe me. I've already gone through my shock-and-awe phase hours ago. I don't cower from shit. I adapt. There's a gang of crazed wolf-shifters hunting me down. That's simply a fact. You and your elite team, who are also shifters, saved my ass—also a fact." A sudden memory struck me, and my stomach plummeted. "Shit. Wait. Did I bend over and tell you to kiss my ass?"

Bear nodded. "Don't forget the part where you smacked your ass like you were a backup dancer at the music awards." He smirked. "I believe there was twerking involved."

"Oh my fucking God." I wanted to bury my head from embarrassment.

Bear went on. "But that was after you smacked me in the face."

"Damn, I would trade my motorcycle just to have a pic of that shit." Grant laughed and then tried to cover it up with a cough.

"Sorry," I replied somberly. "Apparently, I was delirious."

"And I'm the polar bear." Grant winked at me. "You know, the one you petted like a damn puppy."

I groaned inwardly. "Fuck." They must have taken me as a raving lunatic. "Apologies," I mumbled.

"No worries, sweetness. I loved getting stroked by you," Grant replied while wiggling his brows. "It reminded me of this hot chick I knew out in Texas. She liked to—"

I sat up, staring at him, truly interested in hearing where his freaky story was going.

Bear growled at him. "Get your kinky ass out of here, Grant."

Grant smiled. "Hey, there's nothing wrong with a little fur-play."

"Fur-play? Oh, I get it... so..." I grinned at Bear. "You're Grumpy Bear. Grant is Kinky Bear. And Cutter is Clown Bear."

"Hey, I want to be Kinky Bear," Cutter chimed in from out of nowhere.

*Damn, these shifters have very good hearing.*

Grant puffed out his chest. "Sorry, asshole. I got dibs on the nickname."

I bit my bottom lip, fighting the laughter. "So tell me, Kinky Bear, what exactly is fur-play?"

Bear eyed me. "Raven, don't encourage him."

"I'm so glad you asked." Grant grinned wider. "It involves some—"

"I swear, if you don't shut the fuck up, I'm going to claw your face off," Bear hissed.

"I'll tell you later, when Grumpy Bear's not around." Grant wiggled his eyebrows at me again.

Bear's fingers transformed into claws, and Grant scrambled to his feet.

"I've got to go and keep watch with Cutter."

I watched him disappear before glancing up at Bear. The somber expression in his eyes brought me hurtling back to reality once more. "Why are Price and his pack doing this to me?"

"Actually, I was hoping you could tell me. I have some questions for you, but you need to eat and rest. You've been through a lot in the past few days." He reached down to take hold of a thermos and then handed it to me. "Chicken broth."

Taking a large gulp, I groaned, enjoying the scrumptious hot taste. Then I guzzled it so fast I choked.

Bear pressed a thumb against my face. "Slow down, darling."

Taking smaller sips, I drained the contents, loving the warmth that immediately filled my stomach. "Thank you for the broth. But I don't think I'll ever sleep well again."

"There's a nice warm fire, and I'll be by your side the entire night." He watched me with a delicious intensity that made me hot and jittery.

"Why?" My voice broke.

Bear was an enigma I wanted to solve.

Glowering, he demanded, "Why what?"

"Why are you protecting me? I don't even know you." Even though it felt as if I did.

He leaned down and nuzzled my neck. The gesture was familiar and comforting.

His head shot up, and he stared at me. "I'm not certain if you'll understand this," he said while effortlessly turning me to face him with my legs straddling his waist. "But I feel drawn to you, Raven." Bear framed my jaw with his digits.

A delightful tingle raced down my back. His skin was rough with calluses, just the way I loved it. I couldn't stop myself from wondering what those hands would feel like gliding over my skin or sliding between my legs, playing with my hot center. Moisture pooled in my pulsating womanly folds.

Bear's nose twitched before he said, "Bears protect what's theirs." He rubbed a finger across my bottom lip. "And I would fight to my very last breath to ensure you're safe. I just need to know you trust me to do what's right... for you."

I swallowed hard. "I do," I finally whispered, "more than I should."

Staring, mesmerized, I watched Bear lean closer, but then he paused. I could tell part of him was trying to hold back, but I met him halfway. His sinful lips came closer, eventually pressing on mine. My body twitched at the contact. A fire started deep within my gut, spreading throughout my body.

Bear was slow, confident as his tongue swept across my top lip and then my bottom. I opened my mouth, allowing his tongue to slide between my teeth. He tilted his head to the other side, his lips methodically claiming me.

I knew I should pull away, but it was as if I were tethered to him by some invisible string while his tongue curled around mine.

*Damn, he knows how to kiss.*

We both moaned, and his hold tightened on my jaw, pulling me closer. Part of me knew I shouldn't be doing this with Bear, but I wanted to forget about the ugliness—the wolves trying to kill me—just for a second.

I wanted—no, I needed this moment with Bear.

My hands ran up his back, and I felt his muscles jump as I caressed him. He dropped his fingers from my face, and slowly, his digits found their way to my waist, sliding up my shirt. The second his fingers reached my naked skin, I groaned, pressing into him.

This was right. I sensed it in my gut. This was exactly where I was supposed to be.

Bear sucked my tongue into his mouth. My tongue slipped around the tip of his and then rubbed under it. The kiss would've gone on forever if I hadn't attempted to shift more, feeling the stitches tug at my shoulder. I winced, and Bear pulled his mouth from mine, quickly catching my face softly.

"I'm sorry."

"Bear, I'm all right. Really."

His jaw tightened. "I'm supposed to be taking care of you, not pawing you when you're injured."

I leaned forward, nipping his bottom lip before pulling back. "It takes two. And if you didn't notice, I thoroughly enjoyed the hot pawing."

He stood up with me cradled in his arms before kneeling and gently laying me onto a sleeping bag. "You need sleep. In the

morning, you can think about what you want to do next," he told me. "Are you still hungry?"

I nodded. "A little." My tummy growled.

He gave me a big strip of jerky and a bottle of water.

I drooled over the jerky as I took it. "What do you mean about what I'm going to do next?" I bit off a huge chunk and chewed quickly. I'd never been a big fan of beef jerky, but I was starving.

"You can stay here with my men and me, or I can have them take you to safety, and you can be on your way home by lunchtime."

As I was still chewing, my heart skipped a beat as I thought about being separated from him. Plus, something else troubled me. Boyle could have killed me earlier. They all could have, in seconds, right before Cutter and Grant had stepped in.

*So why didn't they?*

I wasn't an imbecile. I recognized something else was going on, and by the look in Bear's eyes, I was right.

I took a huge swig of water. "Bear, this isn't about them killing me, is it?"

Bear hesitated and then shook his head. "No."

My hand clenched around the bottle. "So if I do get out of here, they'll still keep coming after me?"

Anger clouded his eyes. "Yes, I'm certain they would."

Resting the bottle beside me, I asked, "And would I ever see you again?" The thought of never seeing him again filled me with apprehension and desperation.

He reached out, tightly gripping my hand. "Likely not."

I rubbed my thumb over his skin. "Then I'm staying." I kept up a finger, quieting his protest. "And not because I'm helpless."

"Raven, no one ever implied you were helpless."

"I can't explain why, but something's telling me it'll be better if I stay by your side. So I'm going to buck common fucking sense and listen to my gut."

"I can't argue with that, darling," Bear muttered before kissing the crown of my head.

I smiled slightly. "Good, because you wouldn't win."

He chuckled. "Get some sleep. You'll be safe."

"I know." I laid down my head, still holding Bear's hand, and in seconds, I was out.

# CHAPTER 38

## BEAR

I SAT BESIDE HER, watching my dark beauty sleep, as night fell around us. Glancing at her arm with the mark, I wondered when Taggert would get back to me with some information.

There was no doubt in my mind that Raven's parents were Protectors and they had done something really bad to piss off the wolves enough for them to hold a grudge for this long.

"Who are you, Raven?" I asked quietly, pushing strands of hair away from her peaceful face.

Our kiss had been intense and awoken feelings in me I hadn't known existed.

My inner bear growled contently. The beast was becoming attached, and my human side was slowly following. Raven was pulling me in with every second I spent with her. Soon, I wouldn't be able to handle not being near her.

Damn, this was a fucked-up and dangerous predicament.

Why the hell would fate finally bring me my mate, only to have her be a Protector?

# CHAPTER 39

## RAVEN

AIR RUSHED against my face as I dived from the airplane. It was cold, but it didn't bother me as I fell through the sky. I laughed and yelled with delight as I soared in the air.

No wolves were up here trying to kill me. No hot men were turning into killers. Nothing but danger-free air and birds to keep me company. I wanted to stay there forever, just keep falling and never hit the ground.

But the second I touched down, I knew there'd be pain. That was the last thing I wanted to think about right now.

The past few days had been worse than anything I'd ever been through in my entire life. I was being hunted like nothing more than an animal, and then there was the mystery of why these particular monsters wanted me.

No, I didn't want my reality.

I wanted my dream to go on forever, but something shifted beside me, and there was a sudden flood of warmth. The last bits of sleep slipped through my fingers, and I landed back into my injured body.

Still exhausted, I slowly opened my eyelids and nearly jumped out of my skin before I remembered why two grizzly bears and a polar bear were keeping close company beside me.

"Bear?" I inquired.

The grizzly bear nearest raised its head and grunted quietly. I didn't think bears could smile, but this one did. His bulk was wrapped around my side, and his massively large head was right beside mine.

Eventually, I hoped I'd get used to seeing them in this form. Maybe one day.

I quickly figured out Grant, with his stark-white fur, was the polar bear, and Cutter was the other grizzly. Both weren't far away, their backs toward me as they faced the surrounding trees. But this clearing was different.

"Did we move campsites?"

Bear's furry head bowed in response.

"Guess the wolves were getting too close for comfort." I grunted, trying to sit up.

Bear made a low guttural sound in his throat when I winced in pain.

"I'm fine, promise. Just stiff as hell and need to move a bit."

Bear growled, and I felt the rumble go through his chest and down my back. It tickled, so I began to laugh until he tilted his head at me with confusion in his eyes.

"What? I promise. I'm fine. I'm in no shape to do anything crazy."

Bear supported my back with his bulk until I was upright, leaning against his hulk of a shoulder. Speaking of shoulders, mine throbbed, and I could feel the stitches in my skin. It freaked me out, but I wasn't about to admit it to this pack of bears.

*Wait, do they even call themselves a pack? Maybe it's something else altogether? I probably shouldn't mistake them with wolves.*

Bear nudged me gently, and I glowered.

"Just thinking about you is all. You know, about what all this shit means..." I trailed off as I stared into his blue eyes and found myself sinking deeper and deeper into their mesmerizing depths. They were filled with strength, courage, and... *sadness?*

I desperately wanted to know what he was thinking and, more importantly, feeling right then. Our kiss had told me he found me attractive, and he was obviously willing to risk his life for me.

*But why?*

He plunked his head onto my lap. My fingers dug into his soft fur before I methodically stroked him. He huffed deep in his throat, and the sound made my womanhood pulse.

"So do we have a plan, or are we just going to keep hiding out in the woods?" I finally forced myself to ask, just to break the building sexual tension between us.

For a moment, I assumed Bear was going to ignore my question, but then he slowly started to get up, making sure I could support myself. His big form lumbered away, and I heard a large roar that turned into a man's groan. I couldn't see anything through the trees, but a moment later, a black-clad Bear came back to the fire. His whole body was pure rippling muscles, and he had to be at least six three.

*Damn, he's gorgeous. Just plain fucking gorgeous.*

His dark-brown hair was clipped short. His features intrigued me—from his chiseled cheekbones and painfully hard jaw to his searing blue eyes, which made me so horny I wanted to tackle him and ride him like a bucking bronco.

I tried not to get all nervous, like an infatuated schoolgirl, as he sat beside me with his shoulders completely dwarfing mine.

"Sometimes, I forget humans can't communicate like we do." He nodded to the other two bears. "It simplifies things."

"You can talk telepathically?"

He nodded slowly. "As a bear clan, we hold a strong mental connection that unites us as one." He stoked the flame. "Are you certain you want to know what the plan is?"

"Yeah, I'm assuming you fur balls have one."

Bear raised his brows at me. "That's the best you could come up with? Fur balls?"

The other two bears both turned. Grant shook his head as Cutter snorted, but I only grinned wider.

"Yeah. Give a girl a break, all right? I'm tired. I'm injured." I scrunched up my nose. "And I need to wash myself, like stat. I smell like death warmed over. So what's the plan?"

"Honestly, we're still trying to put all the missing pieces together. We have questions, and until I know everything, we're going to keep you alive, since you insist on staying here with us."

My eyes narrowed suspiciously. "You're the one who told me he'd keep coming after me."

"Yes, I did."

"Why would he come after me?" I snapped, losing patience.

He hesitated, and his gaze went to my arm, the one with the birthmark.

I rolled up my sleeve and stared at it. "It's an ugly birthmark. It has zero to do with this."

He sighed heavily. "Actually, it has everything to do with why you're being hunted."

I stared at the mark and then ran my fingers over it. *How could it have anything to do with what's going on?*

"Why were you asking about me being an orphan?" I asked quietly, not sure if I really wanted to know the answer.

He moved a finger over the birthmark. My body twitched at the caress. A piece of me never wanted his touch to stop.

*What the hell is happening to me?*

I'd never felt like this around any man before, and this wasn't the time to be falling for Bear. Besides, love was a distraction, especially when I didn't know what was going on.

His fingers caressed my skin as he gazed at me. "This sign represents something from our world."

My stomach churned. "Am I, like, marked prey or something?"

Bear laughed gently. "Actually, it's the other way around."

My brows furrowed as I glanced at the mark and then back up at him. "You're supposed to be my prey?" My heart raced.

"How in the world would that work? I'm pretty sure you could kill me with one swipe of your giant-ass paw."

He slightly shook his head. "Normal people don't smack bears in the face, Raven. I think, subconsciously, you know what you are, what you're supposed to be doing. I think your mind has been trying to tell you, but you've probably been fighting it your whole life. Plus, you've never had someone to guide you."

I was lost. I sat up straighter and tried to get ahold of the reality that was quickly slipping from my grip. What Bear was implying meant my life was about to turn upside down.

*Do I really want to deal with this shit?*

Getting out of this mess alive and making sure Price and his pack of deranged wolf-shifters never came after me again was my number one priority. I couldn't give a shit about the rest.

"Raven?"

"Sorry. I'm just not sure what you're trying to tell me."

"You never knew your parents or anyone else in your family. But if you had, your life would have turned out completely different."

I sighed. "Well, yes, that's a given. I lived my life in a series of fucked-up foster homes."

"You were born from a long line of Protectors, Raven." He pointed to the mark on my arm. "You were marked from birth as one of them."

Shaking my head, I stood too fast. Dizziness overwhelmed me, and Bear helped steady me.

"Get to the point, Bear."

"Why do you think you chose your profession? Something else is driving you, a voice telling you that you need to be doing something more. Jumping out of airplanes gives you a rush, but it never lasts long enough, does it?"

"Stop it," I whispered. Panic made my heart twist in my chest, and my gut clenched at the truth of his words. I always called myself a thrill-seeker, but maybe something else had been driving me to take bigger and riskier adventures.

"You were born to the Protectors, but they gave you up as a child. You stumbled into this world because of Price, because of what you are."

"Shut up! I'm not a Protector," I cried. "I'm not anything! I'm just Raven!"

Bear only stared as Cutter and Grant glanced over their massive shoulders at our exchange.

*I can't handle this. Accepting there are strange things in the world, fine. I can get over that. Learning I'm supposed to be a part of this insanity, too? Absolutely no way in hell.*

I liked my life and didn't need this shit.

I glanced at Bear's determined eyes. He wasn't going to let me stick my head in the sand and pretend this wasn't happening. His sheer strength and stubbornness were what I needed to face the truth.

He was right. A restlessness always tormented me. I was never really happy or fulfilled.

"The faster you accept what I'm telling you, the easier it will be to fight Price and his pack."

"Oh, hell no. You didn't say shit about fighting," I retorted, still reeling.

He smirked for a second. "You were born to be a Protector, a fighter. You need to embrace that side of yourself, just as your parents did when they were alive."

*Does he know who my parents were?*

A sudden pang in my chest made me want to ask who they were, but it was quickly replaced with anger. They'd abandoned me, and I hated them for it.

"Raven," Bear whispered softly. "Please, sit back down. Your shoulder has to hurt like hell right now."

"It's okay."

"Can you at least sit back down so we can talk?"

"No, I need a minute, all right?" Panic coursed through my veins. "Can I have that at least?" My chest tightened, like I was one step away from hyperventilating.

He gazed at me with those damn beautiful eyes. "Okay, but I can't let you go out there alone."

My body relaxed slightly. "Then follow me, but keep your mouth shut." I turned and walked toward the trees, desperately needing some peace and quiet to gather my thoughts.

I trudged on through the snow and trees with Bear following close behind. My shoulder ached, but I had much more pressing issues on my mind, like accepting the possibility that I was a Protector.

*But of whom?*

# CHAPTER 40

## TAGGERT

GRUMBLING, I stared down at the reports on my desk. We'd finally found what we thought was the last body on Josh Price's land.

The count was too high for me to mentally process. I wanted to find that damn Price and rip out his throat. Children had been among the bodies.

*Kids.*

*What sick bastard could kill that many children?*

Then there was the issue of Armstrong and his team still trying to take the shifter down. This woman he had me checking on had me wondering what I wasn't being told.

I knew Armstrong refused to share some things about his shifter world, and as a human, frankly, I was thankful not to know everything. But as the leader of a top-secret and classified paranormal team, it annoyed me.

It was my job to know what was going on, including why a large gathering was happening at Price's house. The land we'd found the bodies on was owned by Price. However, the house there looked like it was rarely used.

The main house Price lived in had at least thirty cars parked

around it daily. People were moving in and out. Something was happening.

Until Armstrong came clean with me, I was going to sit in my office and try not to lose my fucking temper.

A lieutenant knocked on the doorframe. "Sir?"

I scowled. "Yes, what is it?"

The young man with a buzzed head walked in, laying a file on my already overflowing desk. "We received information back on that woman, Raven Holiday."

I nodded, pulling the file toward me. Throwing it open, I began scanning the information. "You found her parents?"

"It took some digging and maybe a few treats here and there, but yeah, we found them."

"And?"

"Dead. Murdered from the looks of it. Pretty brutal, too."

I flipped through the pages. "If you knew you were going into a dangerous situation that you might not come out of alive, what would you do with your baby?"

The lieutenant frowned. "I'd see it was taken care of, sir."

"Precisely. I think our Raven was saved from a terrible fate. Get Bear on the line. He needs to know this—now."

"Yes, sir." The lieutenant turned on his heel and went to patch the call through.

# CHAPTER 41

## BEAR

I WATCHED Raven lean against a nearby tree, muttering under her breath, but I did as she'd asked and gave her space. The last thing I wanted was to piss her off and have to chase her down again. Part of me argued I should just take her to the nearest town and be done with it, but the bear within me growled and snarled at the very thought.

Leaving her was not an option.

Instinct was starting to drive me, no matter what I'd tried to tell myself. I was never going to be rid of her.

It wouldn't be easy to explain or help her deal with the fact that she was a Protector.

The satellite phone in my back pocket went off, and I extracted it as Raven turned to gaze at me. Turning away, I answered, "Armstrong."

"Taggert on the line for you, sir. One moment," a man on the other end replied.

Seconds later, Taggert came on. "Bear, Taggert here. I have some information for you, but I'm only giving it to you on one condition."

I rubbed my brow and tried not to growl. I'd known Taggert would eventually get smart and start withholding information

from me. But his scheming was going to get him in trouble one of these days, just not this particular one. I needed the information too much to argue.

"What do you want to know?"

There really wasn't that much more to tell. He knew about the Hunt, but I was sure Taggert had already come up with fifty more questions to ask.

"Is there a reason you haven't brought Price in yet?"

The question caught me off guard, and I glanced downward at the snow covering my boots. "Why do you ask, sir?"

"This Hunt business sounds like something you don't want me to be involved in."

"Well, sir, to be honest with you, I have laws I have to abide by as leader of my clan."

After a moment of silence, I heard the sound of ice clinking on the other end. It must have been a tough day if he'd already broken out the whiskey.

"What precisely do these laws mean, Bear? I have a feeling I'll not see Josh Price on my base anytime soon."

"What do you want me to tell you?"

"If I'm not going to see him brought to justice, you swear to me right now you'll kill him so he'll never harm another soul on this damn earth."

I glowered. "I swear it, sir. Can I ask what happened to make you go against your own regulations?"

"Children, Bear!" Taggert yelled. "We found the bodies of children."

"Shit," I whispered. "You have my word, sir. He will never leave my land alive."

"Your land? He's in your territory?"

"I'm pretty sure he's trying to set off a shifter war. Might have something to do with Raven. Can you tell me what you know, or do you want to know something else?" I asked, hoping Taggert heard the lack of patience in my voice.

I was the leader of my clan, and it always grated on my nerves to take orders from someone who wasn't a part of my world. Maybe Taggert was starting to understand that, or, at least, maybe he would back off a bit after we stopped Price—if we stopped Price.

"Got it right here," Taggert announced. "Her parents were murdered, brutally, three days after she'd been given up for adoption. The killer was never found."

*Shit. I knew it.* "Do you know how they were murdered?"

Taggert cursed. "Ripped to pieces by what looked like a wild dog attack. Their bodies were dumped somewhere out in the country, only twenty miles from Price's land."

"That fucker," I barked.

"Bear, what's going on?"

I glanced up to see Raven heading over to me.

When she opened her mouth to say something else, I held up a digit.

I needed to know one more thing from Taggert. "Was anyone listed as a potential suspect in the case?"

Raven tilted her head, confused, and crossed her arms over her chest. I knew I didn't have much longer, and she was going to demand to know what I was talking about.

"Hold on while I check the file."

I heard papers rustling.

"Well, looky here," Taggert finally said.

"What have you got?"

"Boyle O'Brien. You know him?"

I growled as the bear inside me raged, fighting to be let out. My hands curled into fists as I tried to control my temper. The last thing I wanted to do was lose it and shift into my bear in front of Raven. "Dammit! That bastard!"

Raven's mouth flopped open, but she didn't seem scared.

"I want to know the minute anything happens, Armstrong. I'll give you space this time, but I have to know when it happens and if we need to brace for a war. Am I clear?"

"Yes, sir. I'll be in touch. I suggest pulling your people back from Price's house."

"Why?"

"If a war does start"—I watched Raven's brow rise—"you won't want your people caught in the crossfire."

I hung up and tucked the phone back into my pocket. Raven didn't say anything, didn't come out with a million questions. Instead, she just stared at me and waited to see what I would do.

I wasn't certain what to tell her first, if anything. The information Taggert had provided confirmed she was a Protector and her parents had been killed, possibly by Boyle. But someone must have ordered it. Her parents must have killed some prominent wolf-shifters to involve this much effort on the pack's part.

"So," Raven finally said, "are you going to make a girl wait or tell me something?"

"About what?"

She jammed her hands on her hips, staring me down. "Bear, don't even play games with me. I know you were talking to someone important. Who was it? Your pack leader?"

"Bear-shifters live in clans, not packs." *Did I never mention I'm my clan's leader?* I thought about all our conversations and realized I hadn't. Not once had I said anything about me being in charge.

*Do I tell her now?*

The bear in me lifted its head and grumbled. He wanted her to know, needed her to understand, because he desperately desired her. He longed for her to know he could and would protect her with his life.

But I wasn't sure she would like the information—at least, not yet.

"The person I was talking to gave me some information."

Glowering, she asked, "Come the fuck on, Bear. Stop beating around the bush. About what? Price?"

"Actually, no," I remarked, not sure how she'd respond. "About you."

Her face stayed blank. "Me?"

"Yeah. I had him do some digging to see if he could find anything on who your parents might have been. And, well, we at least know for sure they were Protectors. That means, by blood, you are, too."

"And your clan leader is certain about this?"

I nodded, not bothering to correct her about Taggert. "Look, Raven, I know it's a great deal to process, but we truly don't have the time for you to examine and ponder your existence."

It sounded harsh, and I wished I could've recalled my words, but Raven wasn't really listening. She looked past me, as if she were watching some other event unfold, maybe one where she wasn't being chased by shifters.

"Raven?"

"Sorry." She paced through the snow, rubbing her hands up and down her arms—whether out of comfort or cold, I wasn't sure. "What did he say about my parents?"

"Are you sure you're up for it?"

She laughed sharply. "That bad?"

"They were murdered after you'd been given up," I told her. "Ripped apart. The only name found in relation to their deaths is one Boyle O'Brien."

Raven froze, and I observed as her eyes turned even darker in anger. Her hands curled into tight fists, and she turned from me, pacing around in a close circle, mumbling under her breath.

I had a good idea what she was murmuring. After all, she knew Boyle and had probably been nice to him. Now, she knew he'd had something to do with why she was an orphan. It would be enough to piss anyone off.

She stopped pacing and turned to me. The mark on her arm was showing with her sleeve rolled up, and she stared down at it for a long moment before locking eyes with me. "In your plan, will Boyle die?"

"It's a possibility," I hissed.

"Make it a reality," she spewed. "I want him dead. I want them all dead."

# CHAPTER 42

## JOSH

Sniffing the air atop the ridge, I glared down over the trees. The snow made everything stand out in perfect contrast to the white glow. I hoped crimson streaks would soon be in the mix, signifying my plans had worked.

When the war started, once again, the wolves would be on the move to the top of the shifter food chain where we belonged. There was no stopping our plans—unless we couldn't capture Raven.

She was the key to all of this.

If we didn't have her soon, I would be risking my place as pack alpha. I would be labeled a failure in the eyes of the pack, and I'd quickly find myself disposed of. It was no secret that the other wolves of the pack would rather have someone else, someone stronger—Boyle. He'd been the chosen one to replace the last alpha. Only I'd fought off many of the other possible candidates—but not Boyle. No, not the man who'd always been by my side. I'd expected everyone else to try to take my place. Instead, Boyle had bowed a knee to me, something that had never settled well with me.

I knew Boyle was a cunning bastard, simply biding his time to strike, like when I was weak and the pack was ready to turn

on me. That time was quickly approaching, unless I could give my pack the war they'd wanted for decades.

Getting the bears out of the way would be the first step. The rest of the shifters would fall easily after that, if they didn't want to follow the new regime the others and I wanted to establish.

"Josh." Boyle approached, barely bending his head.

"Have you found them yet?"

"The bears covered their tracks too well. We're still hunting."

I snarled, the sound reverberating deep in my chest. "We have to find them, and soon. Elder Tadeo is growing impatient."

"If you'd just let us take her from the beginning," Boyle argued, "we would've already been back home."

"You know why we didn't," I snapped.

Boyle didn't say a word. He'd been against the plan from the beginning. He'd told me if I wanted to start a war with the bears, he would be more than willing to find a way to do it without all this running around shit. He'd wanted to take the damn Protector since the start and not have to worry about drawing out the bears.

We knew Bear worked for some government agency. It was dangerous to involve him in any way when he might have backup. That was the last thing my pack needed.

"If you didn't come up here to tell me you found them," I went on, turning to glare at Boyle, "then what do you want?"

Boyle snarled and took a stride toward me before he drew himself back and bent his head in submission. "I've come to tell you this is a fool's errand. How do we know Bear hasn't already called for reinforcements? He knows we're after the woman, and by now, he probably knows who she is."

Impatient, I narrowed my eyes. "What's your point?"

"We should head home and wait for Bear's clan to make a mistake."

"I will not leave without that Protector."

"You're going to get us killed."

"So be it," I snapped, thrusting forward and wrapping a

clawed hand around Boyle's throat. "If every last one of you has to die, then that's what will happen. We need to get Raven, and we need Bear to start the war."

Boyle grunted under my grasp. "Bear's too smart. He won't do it."

"He won't have a choice." I shoved Boyle away, turning my back to look over the treetops once more. "Get the others. Spread the search wider. We have to find them." I heard Boyle's footsteps crunch through the snow, and I called a warning over my shoulder. "And if you come back without good news, I'll kill you myself."

Boyle huffed in reply as he stalked off through the trees and back down the hill.

# CHAPTER 43

## RAVEN

I felt different. I wasn't sure what had happened during my talk with Bear, but ever since, I'd felt strange, like the blood flowing through my veins was on fire and I could do, fight, or kill anything. It was as if a switch had been flipped the second I learned Boyle had murdered my parents. All my senses had abruptly decided to zero in on that one leering face with the scar that had been haunting me for days.

I was going to make sure my face was the last thing he ever saw.

"Raven? Are you going to come with us? Or do you want to continue your staring contest with the tree?" Cutter called out.

I flicked my gaze around to find Bear was gone, and I was left with Grant and Cutter, both watching me with curious eyes.

"Raven, leave the damn tree alone," Cutter snapped. He came to my side, lightly tugging on my uninjured arm. "Let's go do something. You need a distraction."

"No, I need a shot of vodka," I blurted.

"That won't do shit for you," Grant said quietly. "Hunting might."

"The wolves?" I asked, perking up.

"No, we're hungry," Cutter divulged. "How about an elk?"

I gagged, remembering what the wolf pack had done to the other elk. "As long as it's well done," I whispered, forcing the images out of my mind.

I followed Cutter and Grant into the trees and watched in stunned silence as they boldly stripped and shifted from men to bears.

My lips parted. "You shifters sure don't believe in modesty, huh?"

The cracking and rearranging of their bones should have grossed me out, but I'd seen too much to be affected by it. It was simply another thing to add to my fucked-up-things-shifters-do list. Frankly, Grant and Cutter were magnificent creatures, smaller than Bear but still four times my size easily.

Grant, the polar bear, glanced over his large shoulder and clacked his teeth.

I watched, fascinated, as the two exchanged grunts and huffs, flashing their teeth at each other, until they finally seemed to decide what they wanted to do.

Cutter gave me a light nudge in the leg with his big head.

"No need to shove," I spit out as I began traversing the snow-covered landscape.

It was eerily quiet around us. There were no animal sounds and the wind wasn't howling. The storm had broken. However, the sky was black with dark clouds rolling in closer, meaning more snow was on the way. For now, at least, it was calm.

Our footsteps crunched through the snow as we meandered on, in no real hurry to get wherever we were going. I found their presence comforting. Unlike the wolves, these shifters didn't make the hair on the back of my neck stand on end or my gut clench in apprehension. Instead, I was oddly at peace between them as my hands ran through their fur.

They, in turn, didn't seem to mind me either. Neither treated me like a nuisance, and they'd simply bump me in the right direction when they moved. It felt right to be so near them. It was almost as if I were home.

The thought made me stop suddenly, and the two bears turned to stare at me.

"Sorry. I just thought of something," I whispered.

They continued to watch me. Grant growled at Cutter, and he turned to me, tilting his head.

I rolled my eyes. "I don't speak bear."

Grant shook his head as Cutter plopped his furry ass in the snow and grunted at me. I shook my head and laughed, still having no idea what he was trying to say, but it made me smile. Then I was laughing so hard my sides ached. It had been days since I was able to relax.

It was like I'd known Cutter and Grant my entire life. They felt like family, something I'd never dreamed of having.

# CHAPTER 44

## BEAR

CUTTER KEPT GRUNTING AND SNORTING, making Raven laugh even harder. She didn't realize Grant had disappeared into the trees, shifting back into a man.

I stood a few feet away, observing Raven laughing, and a smile found its way to my lips. The whole time I examined her, I realized I'd never seen her so happy. She was laughing as if she didn't have a pack of wolves trying to hunt her down and kill her. A light shone in her eyes that I could see from even this far away.

I longed to be the man who would spend his life devoted to ensuring her happiness.

"Her smile is a beautiful thing," Grant mused at my shoulder.

"Yes, it is," I whispered, unable to take my eyes off her as Cutter's antics made her fall to the snow, still laughing uncontrollably. "It's nice to see her happy."

Grant grinned at me. "Your mood has changed. Finally, no brooding or sulkiness. And wait... Is that an actual gleam in your eyes? Shit. I haven't seen that in years." He looked back at Raven. "For a Protector, she seems to be quite at home around us. Cutter and I, for a moment, thought we were strolling with a shifter, not a human."

My stomach twisted. "Well, she's not. So what's your point?"

"That perhaps she fits in better with us than I first assumed. She's not just a meddlesome human we have to protect." He scratched his nose and tried to ignore the look I gave him. "Maybe she should stick around for a while."

"Stick around for a while?" I repeated.

Grant nodded. "Just to see how she gets along with everyone... and you."

My hands were suddenly sweaty. I grunted, avoiding the issue, even as my gaze immediately went back to Raven. She was holding Cutter's paw against her palm, her eyes widening as she took in the size compared to her tiny hand. A pang of jealousy shot through me as I witnessed her with another bear, and I flashed my teeth.

I didn't want to have this conversation right now. There was no time for me to try to understand what I might be feeling for Raven. She was a Protector of all things. There was no possible way she'd be accepted by my fellow bears. Just no chance in hell. There was too much animosity and distrust between Protectors and shifters.

"Enough, Grant. We have more important things to deal with right now besides my possible feelings for Raven."

"Possible?" Grant mumbled under his breath as he shook his head. "So fucking stubborn."

I chose to ignore him. "I haven't smelled the wolves in a while. What do you think?"

Grant took a long sniff of the air. "There's no hint of wolf. They must be downwind, or they turned tail and ran. We covered our tracks well." He patted me on the shoulder. "It should give us time to come up with a plan to finish this for good."

I didn't say anything to that either. I knew the only way to draw Price out long enough to attack him would be to use Raven as bait. It was what Price wanted, what he'd come all the way up here for—to get Raven, start a war, and watch the

shifters' world fall to pieces so only the wolves remained on top.

I knew my clan was the strongest among the clans, and we were the only real force that could threaten Price. But I wouldn't go to war alone and risk the lives of the members of my clan.

If Price crossed the line, if he started a war, I would call Taggert in without hesitation in order to keep the situation contained and under control. I'd be damned if I let Price tear this country apart.

"Bear, did you hear me?"

"Hmm? Sorry," I replied, turning to Grant. "What did you say?"

"What should we do until then? We can't just keep wandering through the woods."

"Raven isn't ready to face Price again." I stepped toward her and then stopped. "Her wound is still too fresh, and she doesn't even know how to fight."

Grant nodded. "I agree, but she was at least brave enough to smack a grizzly. It's in her blood to fight. All we have to do is tap into it and help her see her true potential."

I couldn't argue, but still, a part of me didn't want her anywhere near any fighting. I didn't want to see her get hurt again.

As Raven's laugh echoed through the trees, I felt my heart jump, and once again, I found my feet moving toward her. I should've stopped myself, but my inner bear was determined. He wanted to be near her, needed to feel her presence.

I wanted to fight it, but the pull was too strong. I gave in as Grant roared when he shifted back into his polar bear.

"I thought you were going hunting," I growled when I approached Raven and Cutter.

The latter was on his back, Raven scratching his stomach as if he were nothing more than a giant dog. She turned, grinning wide, as Cutter glanced at me with his tongue lolling out of his mouth.

"Cutter."

The smaller bear grunted and then rolled over to his feet as Raven moved aside. He shook out the snow from his fur and then plopped his butt down, waiting for orders. I rolled my eyes at the younger shifter.

Cutter would never grow up. Some days, it would drive me insane. Other days, his lightheartedness would ease the tension and make me glad I'd chosen him as my second-in-command.

"We were just taking a break." Raven smirked. "I guess they felt I needed a little fun. Thank you." She winked at Cutter.

My lips twitched. "I'm sorry about everything you found out this morning. I know it's a fucking lot to digest."

She blew a breath out, nodding, and then laughed darkly. "Yeah, finding out your parents were torn to shreds and you're a Protector who's also about to be torn to shreds... it's a lot to process."

"Raven, I won't let anything happen to you," I promised. I fucking meant it.

"Don't promise anything yet," she whispered. She had an expression of intense thought on her face before she looked away, and then she eyed me. "So are we hunting or what?"

"Hell yes." I started stripping off my clothes, and my inner bear responded with a large roar.

Raven blinked. "Not exactly shy about showing all your junk, huh." It was a statement, not a question.

"Nope. Nudity isn't a big deal for shifters," I replied with a smile. "But you can turn away or check me out. Either way, it's all good, darling." My muscles flexed when I was completely nude.

Raven bit her bottom lip while her eyes roved down my body.

Stepping closer, I softly grabbed her chin. "Like anything you see?"

Her eyes dilated. "Everything."

I smelled the sweet scent of her aroused womanhood.

"Good." I rubbed my thumb across her lips.

Her tongue flicked out, running it over my digit. I shuddered. Soon, I'd get to taste her delicious nectar. Stepping back, I let the shift take over. My skin rippled and my bones shifted and popped.

Raven took a few steps back to watch, open-mouthed, in awe as the monstrous grizzly appeared where I'd been standing just moments before. I licked my nose and then sniffed the air around me, throwing my head up to see what was near. My ears twitched around, and I growled for Cutter and Grant to get moving.

"I'll never get used to that," Raven whispered before I gently nudged her with my head.

Our strange-looking group headed once more into the trees, and Raven's hand found its way into the fur at my shoulder. I felt warmth flood my body. Her touch, that one simple caress, made my bear growl contentedly.

*This is right. She is mine.*

All my worries about what might happen with Price disappeared. Nothing mattered as long as Raven stayed in my life. The realization hit me like a punch to the gut. I paused, paws sinking into the snow, as Cutter and Grant did the same in front of me.

Raven glanced at the three of us. "What's wrong?"

I couldn't answer. I knew Grant and Cutter had heard the thought through our mental connection, and I waited to hear what they would say. To my surprise, neither uttered a word. They huffed at each other and then turned back around and continued.

"Bear?"

I turned my eyes toward hers and stared into their depths. I still needed to tell her so much. Hell, I didn't even know that much about her. In that moment, all I wanted to do was turn back into a man, profess the truth, and take her somewhere quiet where we could be alone and I could finish what we'd started, see where a single kiss could get us.

"Bear, you're kinda freaking me out here." Her grip tightened in my fur.

After another moment, I shook my head and we kept on walking. I tried to keep my thoughts to myself because I knew the others could hear them. We needed to find a distraction before what I was thinking turned into what I hoped might happen.

The last thing Raven needed to hear on top of everything else was that she was my mate.

I was pretty sure I'd get smacked again—hard.

# CHAPTER 45

## RAVEN

AFTER BEAR HAD SHIFTED into his animal form, it didn't take long for us to find a herd of elk. Bear grunted. Cutter lumbered his way back to wait with me as Grant and Bear headed off to get their kill.

For a minute, I thought I wouldn't be able to watch, that it would be like watching the wolf pack kill all over again. But it was entirely different. Grant and Bear worked together as they edged around the herd. When they charged forward, most of the elk took off, but Grant and Bear managed to separate one. When Bear went in for the kill, he aimed for the neck and bit down, and I heard the loud snap. He'd broken its neck. The elk was dead. It was a simple, clean, and humane kill.

I let out the breath I'd been holding and told myself to relax.

Bear dragged the body, and we headed back to our campsite.

Once the three bears shifted back into men and got dressed, Grant went about preparing the elk so Cutter could cook it. They chatted and joked quietly back and forth as I watched, content to be near them with the warmth of the fire in front of me. A knife landed at my feet, and I jumped, looking over at Bear across the fire.

"Let's go," he bellowed.

I stared from the knife to the determined look on his face. "And do what?"

"You need to learn to fight or at least defend yourself."

Gingerly, I picked up the knife and then glanced at the gun holstered at his shoulder. "With a knife? Why can't I just have a gun?"

His lips narrowed to a thin line, but he pulled the handgun out and came around the fire. "Hit the target, and I'll let you use it."

*Easy enough*, I thought, getting to my feet and trading the knife for the gun.

It was big in my small hands, but not uncomfortable. "All right, what am I hitting?"

I looked around at the trees and knew I could make a shot without a problem, until Bear got my attention and pointed to what he wanted me to shoot.

"That? How am I supposed to hit that shit?"

High up in the trees were ravens flying from one branch to another.

"You act like you can shoot. Prove it. Hit a moving target, and then maybe you can have the gun."

I glared at him, and then I raised the gun and aimed. I slowly squeezed the trigger. Three quick rounds popped off. Nothing fell dead to the ground.

*Shit.*

I'd missed the birds. "I can't hit a moving target," I grumbled.

*Damn, this is harder than I thought it would be.*

"Then you can't have the gun." He gently took it from my hands.

"The wolves are bigger targets," I argued. "I could hit them quite easily." *In the head, ass, and flank. I wouldn't miss those fucking shots.*

Bear shook his head as he handed me the knife again and backed away. "Shifters aren't as easy to kill as humans. You have

to hit them in two spots—head and heart—if you want to kill them. Both targets are moving, and both are about the size of those ravens."

Cutter and Grant had stopped their chatting to watch. My fingers twitched nervously as I tried to ignore them. I gripped the weapon in my hand. The buck knife was at least ten inches long. I personally had never used one, but hunters I had taken out on trips used them to field dress their kills.

"So how am I supposed to use this?" I demanded.

"You have to get in close. You won't be able to kill them unless you directly penetrate the heart or brain." Bending his knees, he raised his hands in a defensive stance. "Attack me."

I started to laugh until I realized he was serious. His arms were as big as my legs.

"Oh, hell no. I'm not going to attack you. What if I stab you?"

"It'd be all right with us." Cutter laughed until Bear flashed his teeth.

I looked at the blade in my hand and then the large male in front of me.

*Fine, if he wants me to attack him, that's what I'll do.*

I sprinted forward, raising the knife, ready to stab him in the chest, and then I was suddenly landing hard on my back in the snow.

*Holy shit.* Dazed, I stared up at the darkening sky. "Ow." *This really is going to hurt tomorrow morning.*

Bear held out a hand and pulled me to my feet. "That's what happens when you don't think."

Cutter laughed, but Grant watched pensively.

For the next twenty minutes, Bear worked with me, showing me the proper way to attack someone head on. I spent most of that time on my ass, cursing, but the more I practiced the moves, the more confident I became.

We would have kept going, but Cutter told us the food was ready, and Bear ungraciously let me take a break.

"Shit. I'm pathetic at fighting," I mumbled over a mouthful of elk. I'd never had it before, and it was a bit gamey, but otherwise, it was edible. I was just happy it wasn't raw and bleeding.

"You're a Protector. It's in your DNA to be a skilled fighter. You just need to tap into your inner power," Bear replied.

I scoffed. "Inner power? What am I? Some fucking superhero?"

He stared at me. "You're stronger than you realize. Faster, too." He took a huge bite out of the elk and chewed. "But something's still holding you back."

"Maybe it's because this is all insane to me," I whispered, staring into the night. "I still can't believe I'm a Protector."

According to Bear, I was born into a long line of humans who were bred to hunt down feral or rogue shifters and kill them when they'd become a threat to human society.

"What's so hard to believe?" he asked.

I shot him an annoyed glare. "Uh... I just found out my entire bloodline is a hot mess of killing machines. Where I come from, that shit isn't exactly normal."

"Well, you'd better get over that damn hurdle pretty fast. Otherwise, lights out." His jaw tightened as he glanced down at his plate.

My back straightened. "What aren't you telling me?"

The three shifters glanced at each other over the fire before Cutter snapped, "Bear, just tell her."

"Tell me what?" I asked.

Bear growled. "You're the only way we can get Price out into the open so we can stop a war."

My eyes widened. "You never said shit about a war." *What else don't I know?* "Wait a damn minute. How can I stop a war? I'm not a shifter."

No one added a word, and I got tired of waiting for them to reveal the truth.

I threw my plate into the snow and turned to glare at Bear. "Tell me what the hell is going on."

"You know what's up," Bear responded.

"Obviously, I don't. Tell me now, or I swear, I'll walk the fuck out into the woods and not turn back." It hurt like hell that he didn't trust me enough to be honest with me.

"She has a right to know if she's going to be a... well, you know," Cutter mumbled. Then he immediately buried his face back in his plate.

Grant threw a handful of snow at him and said, "Keep your mouth shut."

I waited, but Bear didn't say anything.

"Okay, I'm done." I jumped up and made for the trees.

If he didn't have enough faith in me to be truthful, then I didn't need to be here.

Bear was at my side in a shot, grabbing my arm. "Raven, wait."

I tried to shake off his hand, but it didn't work. "Get your hand off me, Bear."

Over his shoulder, he barked, "Cutter, Grant, give us some time to talk alone."

Once they cleared out, Bear gently tugged me, but I refused to move.

"Are you going to be honest with me?" I asked.

"Yes."

I allowed him to lead me back to the fire.

"Have a seat." There was a growl to his words. He paced back and forth before me, hands curling into fists.

*Damn, this must be terrible news.* "Bear, just tell me. It can't be any worse than everything else that's going on... Can it?"

# CHAPTER 46

## RAVEN

I STARED into the fire and watched the flames flicker across the logs, consuming the bark and turning it from brown to white ash. That was what I felt like right now, like everything was consuming me, setting me on fire. I'd been firmly sucked into a world I'd never known existed, and now, I was fucking smack dab in the middle of a shifter war.

This was a damn reality show from hell, and I was the lead character.

"Raven, you haven't said anything in a while," Bear whispered. He held my hand as he sat beside me.

We had our backs against a log. My eyes darted to the storm rolling in from the west. It wouldn't hit for another couple hours, but Bear had told me he could already smell it on the wind. It would be rough to get through, but we'd make it.

"I'm just trying to understand."

"Do you need me to explain it again?" he asked gently.

I shook my head. That was the last thing I needed.

Bear had gone through the entire history between the wolves and the other shifters of the world so I could fully understand what Price was up to. That bastard wanted to start a war, and he was going to hunt me to do it. I was going to be the reason Bear

and his family's lives would be put in danger—all because of whom my parents had allegedly killed while they were alive.

*What person wouldn't want to learn all of this in one sitting without a shot of vodka?*

"So I guess we really don't have a choice, then," I finally whispered.

"About what?"

"Using me as bait. We have to stop them. I'm not going to be responsible for starting a war."

"Raven, you're not responsible, and I will not use you as bait."

"Why not? It makes sense," I argued.

# CHAPTER 47

## BEAR

I CLAMPED MY MOUTH SHUT. The answer had almost come out, but I'd stopped it just in time. Maybe when she didn't have a knife still tucked at her side, I'd bring up the whole concept of mates and that I was pretty sure she was mine.

Scrambling for a distraction, I stood up, pulling her with me. "I want to show you something."

She pressed her hands against my chest. "Okay, lead away."

Grabbing her hand again, I snatched my backpack, and we trudged away from the camp and into the forest. It was a comfortable silence as Raven clutched my hand all the way to our destination.

Upon our arrival, she squealed at the scenery—geothermal springs secluded by the forest and stunning mountains.

"Bear, oh my God." Releasing my hand, she jumped up and down with excitement, pointing as the steam hovered over the small cascading waterfall. "A hot spring. I can't believe it." She turned and hugged me tight. "It's beautiful."

"I've never shown anyone this spot. It's my little oasis in the middle of the forest."

She reached up, tracing her fingers along my jaw. "Thank you for sharing it with me." She smiled and then stepped back. "And

just in time. I need to freshen up, like right now." Without pause, she stripped off her boots and clothes before running into the steamy spring. She opened her mouth, gargling the water before spitting it out, the liquid dripping over her delectable body.

I just stood there, gaping, as the moisture trickled down her full breasts.

"Am I going to enjoy this all by myself?"

She didn't have to ask me twice. Dropping my backpack, I kicked off my boots and peeled off my clothes before digging into my bag and yanking out a bottle of Aunt Kristine's specially concocted body wash. Stalking over to the spring, I waded in toward Raven. Squeezing out a dollop of soap, I started to slowly lather her body as the water beat against the rocks. I was pleased that instead of shying away from me, she leaned into my touch.

"You have very skilled hands, shifter." She moaned, not even attempting to move, as I soaped every inch of her stunning body.

"I'm not finished yet, darling." I knelt to wash her legs and feet, and then I circled behind her, lathering her buttocks.

"This is every girl's wet dream." Her eyelids closed.

"I'm here to please," I grunted while pushing to my feet. Then I washed her back and hair.

"My turn?" She turned around and reached for the body wash. "I'll start with the very big parts." She stared pointedly at my hardening shaft.

"Nope. Let me take care of you." I lifted her and carried her over to the huge, flat boulder at the edge of the spring before gathering up her clothes, handing them to her, and heading back over to the water. I made quick work of soaping myself as I watched her, trying to ignore my now hard manhood.

She balled up her panties and bra. "Damn, they're filthy," she mumbled as she stuck them into her coat pocket. She slipped on her clothes and sat upon the boulder. "So tell me about your friends," she said out of nowhere.

This was good. I could talk about them and get the attention off my arousal. "Well, Cutter's like my little brother. He's still a cub at heart."

She laughed. "I can see that. I bet he's a ladies' man."

"He seems to think he is," I replied gruffly. "He's also my second-in-command. We've been close since we were cubs, and he's been there for me every time I needed him. A regular goof, but at the end of the day, he can still kick someone's ass without a problem." I waded out of the water, picking up my clothes along the way.

Her eyes zeroed in on my straining shaft before she loudly cleared her throat. "So there's more to the man behind the smile," she mused, combing her fingers through her hair, untangling the knots.

Standing before her, I put on my garments. "Pretty much." There was no need in telling her behind Cutter's charming persona was a straight-up fierce, ruthless killer who would sacrifice his life to protect me and her... my mate.

"What about Grant? He's hiding something. I can tell."

"Why would you think that?"

"It's how I used to look at myself in the mirror every morning after bouncing around from one foster home to another." Shoving her feet into her boots, she gritted out, "Acting like I was happy when the loneliness and unhappiness were gnawing a hole in my damn stomach."

Moved by the pain in her words, I reached over, running my fingers down her cheek. "Your life seems to have turned out pretty damn good to me." Dropping my hand away, I sat by her side, pulling on my boots.

"Well, yeah, now it is. Not having a family or anyone who gave a shit about me did horrible things to my confidence. There was no 'Team Us.' It was just 'Team Me.' I learned to cope." She shrugged. "So back to Grant. What happened to him?"

My eyes darkened as I remembered a few years ago. Grant

had always been a good fighter and kept to himself, but he knew how to have fun, knew what it was like to be happy.

"He lost someone very dear to him. She was killed by a wolf. Her death nearly destroyed him. I was there for him... helped him pick up the pieces the best he could... but still... something's missing inside him." It filled me with sadness that Grant was now an empty shell.

"That's horrible," Raven whispered. "Was she his wife?"

"More than that, she was his mate. When a shifter finds his mate... it's like finding a lost piece of himself. He feels complete, whole. And when his mate is gone..." I wasn't sure how to explain it, and I fumbled for words. "It breaks most shifters. It's like losing your soul. Grant tries to keep it together, but we all know he's still hurting. He might never recover from it."

"She was his soul mate." Raven bit her bottom lip. "Could he die from a broken heart?"

"No. But it could be a distraction during a battle, so it could get him killed. What's really fucked up is he knows who killed her, but he never talks about it."

Her eyes narrowed. "Price or Boyle?"

"Neither, actually. Maggie. She's a ripe little bitch with a jealous streak. There was a time when our clan and Price's pack got along. That was before Price took over as alpha. Maggie liked Grant, and though wolf-shifters normally never mated with bear-shifters, she convinced herself he would take her as his mate." I left out the part that it didn't hurt that Grant's family was very wealthy and prominent in the shifter community. "Then Grant found his mate, a bear-shifter, in another clan. Maggie couldn't take it. Now I hear she clings to Price's side, hoping to be his mate and alpha-female of his pack."

Raven nodded. "It makes sense. Maggie was always close by Price's side, her gaze never straying very far from him. She looked like a lost puppy most of the time."

"After his mate died, Grant changed. He went from being a fighter to a coldhearted killer. He's the deadliest man I know,

shifter or otherwise. Every time I see him take a life, I remind myself how lucky I am to be on his side."

Raven shivered next to me.

"He would never harm you, Raven."

She rolled her eyes. "I know. I'm not scared of Grant, but what you told me explains the sadness in his gaze when he looks at me. Damn, I just hope he finds love again." She looked at me. "What about you?"

Her question made me growl. "What about me?"

She laughed. "Oh, I see. Not used to talking about yourself?"

She read me well. "No, I usually keep to myself."

The power of being the alpha of my clan was often lonely, even with a ton of bears living around me. I was always worried about the well-being of my clan, from their protection to their survival and growth. Money was never a problem. We had plenty of it, and every member had a share in the billion-dollar corporation my parents had started before they died. The isolation my position brought me and the fact that I didn't have a mate to confide in, to love, and to help strengthen the clan made my status as alpha stifling at times.

"Oh, come on. There has to be something you can tell me," she said, nudging my arm. "Do you have a mate?"

The bear inside my head roared at the word, but I told him to shut the hell up. "No," I replied tightly. "Cutter would love it if I did, though. It would free up some of the ladies who tend to hang on me."

Raven laughed. "Ah, so you charm them with your good looks and then leave them behind." She winked at me. "So you're the fuck 'em and leave 'em Bear."

"No. I just haven't found the right woman yet." I lied through my teeth.

We sat in comfortable silence with only the noise from the trickling spring. A chilly breeze blew by, and Raven shivered. Instantly, I wrapped my arm around her shoulders, pulling her in close. She snuggled up against my side. Every nerve in my body

screamed for me to kiss her, to tell her the truth, but I couldn't, not yet. There was enough on her mind, and telling her she was my mate would only add to all the distractions.

"What do you do in this job of yours?" she asked. "It doesn't sound like a dream job if you're never home."

"I hunt shifters that step out of line," I replied.

My thoughts drifted back to when I'd first started working for Taggert. The number of dangerous shifters in the world that the government tracked was extraordinary, and I'd been put to work with my chosen members of my team to hunt them down and either quietly dispose of them or bring them in.

"Many of my kind feel humans are beneath them. Easy prey. My job is to take down those shifters."

"Josh Price," she whispered as she pressed herself closer to my body.

"He is one shifter I will gladly kill when the time comes."

"He must have done some pretty fucked-up things."

I didn't want her to know how horrible my kind could be, but I wasn't going to lie to her about this. "The Hunt has been going on within Price's pack for a very long time. The man I work for has a team currently digging up bodies on Price's land. Hundreds of bodies. Of all ages."

Raven glanced over at me. I knew she could see the anger building in my eyes.

"He's killed children?"

"His pack has killed children. That's why I have to kill him. He can't keep doing this. If he starts a war, the casualties against other shifters and humans will be worse than anything you can imagine." I hoped she couldn't hear the sadness in my voice, pain I'd tried to keep hidden for many years. I looked away from her intense gaze.

She scrambled onto my lap, facing me, with each knee draped on either side of my waist. "Bear, why do you hate him so much?" She placed her small hands against my cheeks. "What did he do to you?"

I glanced down at her, feeling my heart tear just a little more at the loss I'd suffered. "It's not him I hate. It's shifters like him who think they can do whatever they want without repercussions." I swallowed over the lump in my throat. "My sister... she was killed by a rogue wolf-shifter," I whispered. "She was young, barely eighteen, when he kidnapped her and killed her."

Raven rested her hand on my chest. "I'm so sorry."

"I got the bastard who did it, but ever since... there's been a gnawing anger in me that I can't get rid of. No matter how many shifters I bring down, the anger remains." *Unless I'm around you*, I wanted to say.

Ever since Raven had come into my life, I'd noticed the usual burning rage diminishing. It was still there, but it didn't distract me as much, which made me able to focus.

"I'll help you stop Price," she gritted out fiercely. "You have to let me help you."

"I can't do that," I growled. "I won't risk losing you, not now."

Her face scrunched in confusion. "What do you mean not now?" She softly grabbed my face. "Bear?"

I tried to come up with something to say, but then I scented Grant and Cutter making their way back toward us... just in time to save me from myself.

# CHAPTER 48

## GRANT

CUTTER and I had picked up on Price's scent, but he and the rest of the mangy mutts seemed to be a few miles away.

"We'll be safe for another night, but we'll have to move come morning or risk being caught off guard," I announced to Cutter.

"Exactly." He nudged me. "Do you think Bear has told her everything?"

I shrugged. "I'm sure he's telling her what she needs to know."

I knew Bear didn't want to admit the truth yet, but he wouldn't be able to ignore it forever. Raven was our alpha's mate. Cutter and I could see it plain as day.

"Well, the sooner he says it, the sooner I can get back to being the lone bear on the prowl." Cutter puffed out his chest and grinned. "You could always try to find another mate, too, you know."

I growled, reaching around and grabbing Cutter by the collar. I opened my mouth to snarl at him and then stopped. I forced myself to calm down as I released him. "Sorry. I don't know what I was thinking."

Cutter readjusted his shirt and then rested a warm hand on my shoulder. "I know, Grant. I know."

No, he didn't know. No one knew the emotional pain I lived with every day. A piece of me would be missing forever.

We walked toward Bear's scent in silence, but my mind raced with fear. Sometimes, I felt like I was on a one-way track to going feral. The entire bear clan knew I struggled with my temper and with the idea of trying to find another mate. Unless the right shifter came along, I would continue to grow worse each day. Eventually, I could turn wild, like so many other shifters who had become so heartbroken they couldn't retain their sanity.

When we cleared the tree line, we both paused to stare at Bear and Raven at his secret spot. She was sitting on his lap with her legs straddling his waist, but they were arguing quietly. About what, I wasn't sure, but I had a feeling it was just getting interesting. I could smell the rise of annoyance coming from Raven.

"Are we interrupting?" Cutter asked loudly.

Startled, Raven scrambled off Bear's lap and stood straight up. Cutter hopped onto the boulder, snuggling against Bear's other side.

The alpha growled and nudged him off while I stood before them.

Cutter jumped up, muttering, "Fine. I see how it is. I'll just go stand over here and freeze my ass off."

"It'll be good for you," Bear growled.

Raven laughed while shoving her hands into her coat pockets.

"Did you pick up anything?" Bear asked.

"Price is a few miles out." I checked my sidearm and then my two knives. "We'll be fine through the night, but I suggest we don't stay at the camp too long."

Bear nodded. "We'll move in the morning, and hopefully, by then, we'll have a plan."

Raven glared at Bear. "We have a plan. I'm the bait. I'll draw them out, and then you'll kill them. End of story. I'll be saved, a war won't happen, and we can all go home happy. Right?"

Cutter and I glanced at Bear and saw the frown on his face. Whatever Raven thought the plan was, she apparently didn't realize the full situation. Bear hadn't said a damn thing about her being his mate. Cutter and I knew it was going to be a hell of a lot harder to persuade him to let Raven be the bait.

I sighed, reading the look on Bear's face. He wanted to say no, but unless we came up with another way to lure Price out into the open, Raven would have to be the lure. If Bear lost her, though, I knew it would end him.

# CHAPTER 49

## BEAR

BACK AT THE CAMPSITE, I listened to the three of them go back and forth, and it felt like a bad dream. I wanted to interrupt, but I had to be careful how I showed my authority. Raven still didn't know I was the alpha, and it was getting extremely difficult not to stand up and growl at them, especially when each plan came back to the same issue—drawing Price out into the open. Each time, all they could come up with was using Raven as bait.

"I don't know why we're still discussing this," she muttered, rubbing her forehead as if a headache were blooming. "Just let me do it. Grant will be within feet of me, so if anything happens, he can grab me and get me out of there."

"That's not the problem," I said darkly.

She jumped to her feet and jammed her hands on her hips. "Then what the hell is it?"

I racked my brain, trying to think of an obvious answer. "You're human. You can be easily killed. I can't have you out there running around, risking your life, and probably getting in the way." My words were harsh, but I hoped they worked.

She needed to understand this was dangerous. She might not make it out alive.

My jaw tightened. She was spitting mad.

"Raven, please."

"Please, what?" she snapped. "I survived with these bastards for days. And as you keep reminding me, I'm a Protector or whatever, so this is what I'm supposed to do. It's in my blood to take these fuckers out!"

"Yes, but you haven't had enough training. You could be killed."

Her eyes widened. "Oh, I see. You're just worried I'll distract everyone, that you'll be so focused on me that you'll let your guard down."

*Shit. Yes, that's exactly it.* I shook my head. "No, that's not it. You're fragile."

She barked out a laugh. "Fragile, am I? Who in this damn camp smacked a bear in the face?" She raised her hand.

Cutter laughed until I shot him an evil look.

"Not the fucking point, Raven. Just please, will you let us come up with a different plan?" I said.

"No, I will not. This plan makes sense. So what aren't you telling me? What is it, Bear?"

"What do you mean?" I asked, trying to sound oblivious.

"You're hiding something. What is it? What are you so afraid of?"

"Can't I be worried about you getting hurt?" I asked, losing my patience with this whole conversation.

My inner bear snarled and growled, wanting me to tell the truth, but I fought it.

"No, because it's not just that. What's the fucking issue?"

"It's not the right thing to do—"

"Yes, it is! They want me. I can stop a war. I can prevent hundreds of shifters from needless deaths."

"No, Raven. Just leave it at that."

"I'm doing it, Bear," she argued, stalking around the fire toward me. "I'm going to do it, and you can't stop me." At the last few words, she poked me in the chest with her finger.

"I said no, and that's final," I barked.

"Yes, I am."

"I will not risk the life of my mate!" I finally yelled.

Everyone around me stiffened as an uncomfortable hush fell over the camp.

The second I realized what I'd just shouted, I couldn't even look at Raven. I didn't want to see her sudden rejection or the fear on her face from my words.

Cutter whistled as Grant cleared his throat, crossing his legs at the ankles. The two watched, waiting to see who would move first—Raven or me.

The first was still armed with the buck knife, and I wanted to go hide under a large boulder and maybe hibernate there for a year or two.

# CHAPTER 50

## RAVEN

BEAR and I stayed rooted where we were. I was looking up at his red face in stunned silence.

*Mate? Did he really say mate?*

*No, I couldn't have heard him right.*

"Did you just call me your mate?" I finally forced myself to ask.

Bear cleared his throat. I'd never seen him this nervous.

"If I said no, would you believe me?" His eye twitched.

"No," I answered immediately as I took a step backward. "Mate? But that's what Grant had, right? With the connection and the whole... Holy shit," I whispered, quickly sitting on a log. "Mate? I can't be your mate. I don't even know you."

Cutter said, "Well, for starters, he's the alpha of our bear clan, and—ow!"

Grant reached over and smacked Cutter upside the head, but it was too late.

"What?" Cutter snapped. "She said she didn't know anything about him."

"Doesn't mean you had to tell her, you halfwit. Come on."

Grant grabbed Cutter by the shoulder and dragged him away.

I sighed with relief when they walked away from the camp.

Bear and I needed a few minutes of privacy—or at least some time for me to start screaming at him without interruption.

I was still sitting on the log, looking like I'd been sucker-punched in the gut. There had to be an easy button or a book I'd forgotten to read at some point in my life, anything that could've told me why all this crazy shit was happening to me now, in the middle of fucking nowhere.

This was the last straw. I was pretty sure if I learned anything else, I'd snap, crackle, and pop.

"Raven, I'm sorry I didn't tell you." Bear walked over to me.

"About which part?"

"Both. I didn't want you to be worried about me being the alpha of my clan after your experience with Price."

I laughed bitterly but still didn't meet his gaze. "And the second?"

"I wasn't sure of our connection until you were wounded. I felt your pain, and I couldn't stand it," he growled.

I finally looked up. My heart nearly stopped at the emotions in his eyes—hurt, despair, and fear. It was killing me to see him this way, but I didn't know how to fix it.

*Dammit. Why do I suck so bad at this communication shit?*

I just sat there quietly, not uttering a sound.

After a while, as if he couldn't stand the silence any longer, he sighed. "Listen, it doesn't mean anything. You can still go home when this is all finished, and I won't ever bother you again."

His words were like a stab to the gut. It would slowly kill me to know my mate was out there, and I wasn't with him.

Bear started to walk away.

I reached out, snatching his hand. He turned back to face me.

"Don't," I whispered, looking into his eyes. "I've dreamed about you for months."

He blinked in confusion. "What?"

Tightly gripping him, I pulled myself up, my chest brushing against his. "This is going to sound crazy, but the dreams started

a couple months ago. Each one was with you as a bear and me being stuck in some fucking ice, screaming for help. You would bound out of the forest, always angry and growling." I shrugged. "I thought you were trying to kill me. Now I know better. It was a sign." I paused. "What I'm trying to say is you're not the only one who feels something, Bear."

I swallowed hard. My heart was beating as if I'd run a marathon. "I just wasn't about to call you my mate. Shit. I was just too scared to even call it what it is."

Bear's other hand landed on my hip, tugging me closer to him. "You don't have to do this."

"I'm not trying to make you feel better. It's the truth," I assured him. "The whole time I was out there alone, I knew someone or something was watching over me. I could feel it. Then, when I finally realized who you were after, you saved my life. I feel something I never thought I would feel for anyone. And frankly, it's fucking scary."

My whole life, I'd searched for that one person I knew would love me forever, someone who would be there for me when I needed him, someone who would keep me safe, a man I could act like myself with and have no worries that I'd somehow chase him away if I revealed my inner demons.

Over the past couple years of failed relationships, I'd given up hope that I'd find the right man. It was depressing to think I'd eventually have to settle for the next best thing. Never in my wildest dreams had I thought I'd find the real thing—a man who, when I looked into his eyes, I could see the passion and fire I'd been praying to find.

*Who knew he'd be waiting for me on a life-or-death chase?*

"And who would have thought I'd find the man of my dreams and a furry pet at the same time?" I grinned at him.

He grinned back. "Smartass," he said before his mouth crushed mine.

His tongue thrust forcefully between my lips, sweeping against mine. The kiss was dominant as he took the response he

wanted, demanding my complete submission. One hand possessively collared my throat as his other clutched my ass.

I couldn't get enough of him. I was grinding against him until he hoisted me up, curving my legs around his hips. Helplessly, I moaned with pleasure into his mouth, digging my nails into his back.

Bear broke away from our kiss for one second, his eyes darting around as if he were making sure Cutter and Grant were nowhere close. Then he stared at me with eyes that had taken on a glazed, hungry look, which both thrilled and startled me.

"There's no tent," he groaned as if in agony. "Shit. I don't want our first time to—" His voice croaked before he leaned down, gripping the flesh of my throat between his teeth.

My core pulsated as I reached up, sinking my fingers into his hair, pressing him farther into my neck. "Bear, I don't give a shit about a tent. Just fuck me like a recently released prisoner."

All the blankets were piled near the fire, which was still going strong. Plus, the small clearing of the campsite was secluded, surrounded by trees on three sides and a cliff face on the other. No one would see us.

He straightened before crouching down, slowly placing me on the blankets. My pulse raced while he knelt before me. Impatiently, his big hand yanked my coat, tossing it aside. Leaning forward, I hungrily touched my lips to his before clawing at his jeans, wanting them off. The burning need to have him filling me raced through my veins.

Quickly, I undid his belt, unzipping his jeans. I loved that he was commando.

"Damn," I whispered, pulling out his rigid flesh. I slid my fingers up and down the hot, smooth engorged girth with a slow and steady motion. I was desperate to explore the entire length of his throbbing manhood with my tongue.

"No, not yet, darling." He pushed me back against the blankets and slowly undressed me, leaving me naked.

He stared down at my full breasts and rock-hard nipples with

a seductive smile as his fingers shifted into claws. He paused, as if waiting for me to tell him to stop, but I watched, fascinated. He lightly ran them down the slope of my right breast, and I shivered at the scrape against my flesh. My eyes closed as the sensation rocketed down to my moistness.

My eyes opened again. "Bear," I whispered, watching his claws transform back to a hand.

He straddled me, kissing his way down my neck before sucking one breast while his hand teased the other. I groaned as he inched down my body, leaving trails of fire across my skin.

I had to be dreaming. These feelings—lust, ecstasy, and happiness—couldn't be real. My body was already reaching its high point, and he hadn't even penetrated me yet.

"God, you're the most ravishing creature I've ever seen," he whispered as he nuzzled my hip.

"Have you seen a lot, then?" I asked, smirking.

"Smirk all you like," he murmured. "Soon, you won't be able to."

I smiled wider. "I'm not scared—" I swallowed the rest of my words when his hand glided up my inner thigh.

One finger found my wetness ready and waiting for him. It slipped inside, and I was lost with that one touch. He found an easy rhythm that drove me insane with need. Just when I was on the edge, he pulled his finger out and replaced it with his mouth. He sucked my warm, damp entrance, making me squirm.

"Bear, wait. Not yet, dammit," I breathed.

He glanced up with my wetness glistening all over his perfect lips. "Why?"

"I just want you to know you and I..." Tears welled behind my eyelids. I was overwhelmed by the intense connection I already felt with him.

I wasn't naive, and I knew it wouldn't be easy, learning about his world, but I was determined to work at being everything a woman—a mate—had to be. Now that I had him, I couldn't imagine my world without him in it.

"I'm in this for the long haul," I said in a hushed tone, meeting his gaze.

His eyes burned with passion and affection, something I'd thought I'd never see in any man's eyes for me.

"You are mine, my mate," he growled, "and when I'm done with you, you'll crave my touch and want no one else." Pressing my legs wide open, he took my swollen clit into his mouth, tonguing it, sealing his lips around the flesh, applying just the right amount of suction to bring me to the brink.

I screamed in pleasure as my body went rigid. After swiping his tongue over me, he stood and removed his shirt and boots. When he slid his pants down, I smacked my lips, watching his thick length bob against his navel.

My womanly folds creamed, knowing I'd done this. I'd made this exquisite, strong man ache to be inside me. Reaching up, I grabbed his hard cock.

"Bear," I murmured before my greedy tongue licked the glistening bead off his tip.

"No," he hissed. "Our first time will be all about you."

He smoothly pushed me onto my back before leaning over me. His lips latched onto mine. His tongue plundered and licked me until I was a throbbing mess of want. My body was on fire with a lust I'd never felt in my entire life. All I wanted to do was fuck him like we were untamed animals.

I wrapped my legs around his hips, and he rolled me on top of him. My hand reached down, grabbing him, and I ran my fingers up and down his slick shaft.

I wanted him inside me so deep that I wouldn't know where he stopped and I began. "Do you have a condom?" I uttered. "Just for the record, I haven't been with anyone in a while, and I've been tested for sexually transmitted infections."

He reached one hand up, tracing a finger along my jaw. "Shifters don't carry human diseases, but I want you to be at ease during our first time. Reach over and grab that backpack to your right."

His other hand securely held my waist as I seized it.

"Check the side pocket," he instructed.

Unzipping it, I pulled out a strip of condoms, tossing the bag aside. "I don't know whether to be ecstatic or perturbed that you have so many."

He chuckled. "That's Cutter's backpack and stash. I've been celibate for a long time, darling."

Carefully ripping open a packet, I pulled out the condom as I said huskily, "Well, shifter, I'm going to rock your world."

Massaging his hot, smooth column of flesh between my fingers, I pinched the tip of the condom and rolled it on the swollen head. Slightly rising, I lowered myself onto his molten, thick manhood in one swift movement. My wetness snapped around his girth like a vise. A pulsating energy shot through my body when his hands gripped my hips. With my every downward motion, he pushed up into me.

Our breaths were ragged as we hissed, panted, and grunted in synchrony to the primal slapping of our bodies against each other, seeking our release.

My nails dug into his shoulders, and suddenly, Bear groaned, pulling free of me. He flipped me over, tugging my ass into the air. He plunged into my slick heat from behind and then took me hard and fast. My fingers clawed into the blankets.

On a moan, I begged, "Bear, harder." Little sobs of pleasure came from me.

Bear's fingers stroked my clit in tight, fast circles.

"Oh God, I'm going to come!" I screamed while he slammed into my sex, my body shaking from his forceful thrusts.

He grabbed the back of my hair, arching my body up, and then each of his thrusts came harder and faster than the last. He kissed my neck as his movements became slower, methodically hitting my G-spot with a precision that was fucking diabolical. My toes curled and my stomach tightened.

"Are you mine, Raven Holiday?"

"All yours," I hissed. "Now move that huge cock of yours faster."

He laughed. "Your wish is my command." He nipped my shoulder before hammering in and out of me, rocking me hard.

My channel contracted, and my inner muscles trembled before I cried out, "Bear. Mate."

"Mine," he grunted before groaning and repeatedly thrusting into me.

He poured his seed inside me as his movements became disjointed and he lost his rhythm. He hugged me tight before rolling me over, and I made a small *oomph* sound as my hip hit the blankets.

"Damn. That was fucking incredible," I whispered when I was finally able to form words. My body tingled all over, and everything from my waist down was still reeling with aftershocks. "Just... holy shit."

"Yeah," Bear replied. "That about sums it up."

"Is it like that every time?" I croaked.

He chortled, pulling me even closer before kissing the top of my head. "God, I hope so."

My hand stretched down to caress his already hardening maleness. "Well... there's only one way to find out," I said before nipping his bottom lip.

"I do love a challenge," he declared before moving me onto my back.

No matter what happened next between Price's pack and Bear's clan, in this moment, I knew this connection between Bear and me was right. He was meant to be mine, and I was meant to be his. Without a doubt, we would keep each other safe or die trying.

# CHAPTER 51

## RAVEN



"So explain to me what this whole mate thing is actually about?" I asked a few hours later.

We'd made love several times by the fire until it'd died down enough that Bear needed to build it back up. We'd gotten dressed because we had no idea when Grant and Cutter might decide to return. I really didn't want to be naked when they came back.

Bear was reclined against the log, with me curled up in front of him, leaning into his chest. "What do you want to know?"

"Is there some crazy bear ritual we have to do?"

He rested his chin on top of my head. "I have to claim and mark you at some point."

I scrunched up my nose. "Is that like a golden shower? Are you going to make it rain down on me?"

He replied, "Not," as he chuckled. "It's a bite that goes on your shoulder. It lets others know you and I are mated for life and we are one. It also warns them there will be hell to pay if they fuck with you."

"In other words, you'll rip their damn throats out."

"To say the least." He tightly hugged me for a minute and then sighed. "Being my mate also means being in charge of my

bear clan. It's a lot of responsibility, and their well-being is vital. We're a big family, and we have each others' backs at all times. I also make sure everyone is financially secure. My parents created a corporation years ago. It started out small, but now its assets are in the billions."

I whistled. "Billions? How do you manage a billion-dollar company when you're out here, hunting down rogue shifters?"

"Most of the members of my clan work as employees in some capacity, and everyone owns shares in the corporation. It's really a family-run organization. Before I became alpha, I was pretty hands-on, even lived in Manhattan while working at our head-quarters, but it was driving me fucking insane, being a bear caged in the city. So when my uncle—the former alpha—died, it was a no-brainer for me to come back to the clan and assume the alpha position. I went through a series of challenges with members of the clan before I earned the position, though."

"Challenges? As in actual fighting? I thought you were a family?"

"We are. Shifters respect power, intelligence, strength, and leadership. You can't just demand to be alpha. You have to earn it."

"So as alpha-female, I will be challenged, too?"

His body stiffened. "Fuck no. Not in my clan. In other clans and packs maybe, but not in mine. Shit, they've been waiting for me to find a bear mate for years."

I bit my bottom lip. "But I'm not a bear. I'm human—a damn human who has Protector lineage."

"I'm not going to lie. It won't be easy for everyone to accept our mating, but we'll make this work, Raven. You're my mate, and I will never give you up."

Tilting my head back, I looked seriously into his eyes. "I have one more question about this mating thing."

"Anything."

"Will it hurt?"

"What do you mean?"

"When you bite me?"

Bear burst out with laughter. "Only a little bit."

I rested my head against him and closed my eyes, trying to imagine what it would be like to meet all the other bears.

*Family. I will actually have a damn family.* The thought excited and filled me with fear.

*Will they even like me?*

I was human and a Protector.

I didn't know much about the shifter world, but I was pretty sure that wasn't a good combination.

But I didn't give a shit. Bear was mine, and I'd be damned if I let anyone chase me away.

He said quietly, "I will forever be yours, and you will forever be mine. I will protect and love you for all our lives, and I'll never let any harm come to you. That is my oath as your mate."

There was such tenderness in his words that I felt my heart reaching out to him. Our connection was strong. It was as if I could physically touch it, hold it in my hands, and maybe even follow the connection back to him.

"As it is my oath to you, Bear." I tilted my head back enough so I could see him.

He leaned down to firmly kiss me on my lips. Breaking the kiss, I turned around and straddled his hips. Grant and Cutter catcalled and whistled behind us, making Bear turn and growl, but I only laughed.

"What? We gave you, like, four hours." Cutter joined us at the fire with a toothy grin. "Glad to see you're both still alive. Pay up, Grant."

Turning to sit between Bear's legs, I glanced between the two shifters and watched as Grant grunted and then pulled a few bills from his wallet before handing them to Cutter.

"You made a bet?" I asked.

"On what?" Bear asked.

"On whether or not she would stab you first," Grant asked. "You let me down, Raven."

I laughed. "I claimed him. He's mine. I wasn't about to put holes in him."

"I'm dealing with teenagers," Bear muttered, glaring at Cutter and Grant. "Did you at least do anything useful while you were away?"

"We found a new place to make camp. I suggest we move there." Grant's eyes turned dark. "There's wolf stench in the air. I don't like it. It's too close for comfort."

I felt Bear stiffen before he shot to his feet, pulling me up with him. "Let's get packed up."

It wasn't hard to get our packs ready to go. We put the fire out, and then our campsite looked as if no one had been there for days.

Grant and Cutter shifted to scout ahead, leaving Bear and me to follow close behind.

# CHAPTER 52

## BEAR

THE NIGHT CLOSED in around us and the wind picked up. The storm was ready to break at any time, and I hoped we'd reach the new campsite soon.

Raven held my hand throughout the whole trek. I enjoyed it and would gently squeeze it every now and then to make sure it was real, that she was really beside me as my mate.

I hadn't marked her yet, but there'd be time for that later, if we made it through the next few nights alive.

"Who were you really talking to this morning?" Raven asked.

I was pulled back to the moment. "When?"

"This morning. I asked if you were talking to your alpha, and you said yes. Obviously, you lied." Lightly poking her tongue into her cheek, she asked, "Who was it?"

"Taggert. He's technically my human alpha."

She arched a brow. "Your what?"

"I work for a top-secret branch of the military. Taggert's in charge of me and my team. I've been keeping him up to date on the situation here with Price." I hesitated for a second. "He's the one who tracked down the information on your parents."

She slowed down for a second and then shrugged. "Well, I

guess you had to find out somehow. After a while, I gave up wanting to know anything about them. So... moving right along."

"Are you upset?"

"What? Oh, hell no. Why would I be mad that you had the government secretly dig into my life behind my back?" she bellowed. Then she lowered her head and sighed. "Listen, I'm a little annoyed, but it's fine, really." Her face scrunched up like she was about to punch me.

"If you say so," I replied.

"I do. I would have done the same thing if I were in your shoes." She bit her bottom lip. "As long as Taggert doesn't use it against me or recruit me to work with you on missions like these, then yeah, I'll be just fine."

"Shit." I skidded to a stop. My stomach plummeted at the thought of Taggert asking her to go on missions.

She stopped walking completely. "Bear? Are they going to try to recruit me?"

*Over my fucking dead body.*

"No, of course not," I said too quickly. "They might bring you in to ask a million questions about Price and his pack, but that should be it."

"Dammit, Bear," she yelled. "I will not be some government pet project."

"Listen, I won't let Taggert or anyone else take you away from me." I pulled her hand to my lips and kissed it before I towed her along again. "It'll work out, and besides, Taggert's a pretty nice guy... once you get to know him—for a couple years."

Raven laughed as we caught up to Cutter and Grant. "You're just making it worse. You know that, right?"

I nodded and started to say something else, when I noticed Cutter and Grant had come to a complete stop. There, in front of us, was the entrance of a cave.

I stared at them with a raised brow. "A cave? Really?"

They growled quietly over their shoulders, and Raven dutifully turned around so they could shift back.

She shuddered at the sound of popping bones. "I'm fucking thankful I will never have to deal with shifting. Out of everything else I've seen, that still creeps me out."

I tugged their clothes from a bag and tossed them over. After a minute, I told Raven it was safe for her to turn around.

Cutter directed to Grant, "Told you he wouldn't like it."

Rubbing the back of my neck, I replied, "Of course I don't like it. It's a trap. We'd have nowhere to go if they came here."

"Not true. I scouted it out the other day," Grant said. "There's a second entrance. The cave follows the hill up and comes out on a plateau, which leads to a drop-off, a very high drop-off."

My jaw tightened. It had the potential to be a good trap for Price and his pack. We could easily draw them in on one side and use the drop-off to kill them. If the fall were high enough, no shifter could survive a broken neck or that many broken bones.

It just might work, but I'd still have to hear the plan.

I set down the packs and turned to Raven. "There is no way in hell you're getting involved in this shit."

The reaction from all three of them was instantaneous. Cutter huffed, Grant muttered under his breath, and Raven rolled her eyes.

She jammed her hands on her hips while tapping one foot. "We went over this, Bear. I'm going to be the bait. It's the only way to draw Price out to where we need him."

"I don't care. I'm not risking you now that I know you really are my mate," I roared. "It's not happening."

"She's the best chance we have," Grant argued.

"No. I won't allow it," I barked.

Raven nudged me in the side. "You're being fucking ridiculous. If I'm your mate, that means, technically, I'm also in charge of this clan, right?"

I stiffened. "I don't see what that has to do with anything."

"It means, first of all, I'm at your side, and you can't order me

around," she bawled. "And second, it means what I say matters. And I'm going to be the bait whether you like it or not."

I gripped her shoulders, pulled her close, and bent down so I was eye level. "Hell no, I'm not risking your life."

"But it's okay for you to risk yours?" she shot back. "You're just as likely to get hurt tonight."

I released her and crossed my arms over my chest. "I can take care of myself."

She rolled her eyes. "So can I."

I flashed my teeth that had grown into canines in my annoyance. "No, Raven, I'm not letting you be put in danger, not after I've finally found you."

She didn't understand that finding a true mate was like finding a needle in a haystack. Shifters would search a lifetime for something that was impossible, and many would just grow weary and settle for a warm body and sexual satisfaction. This was the real deal. My future with Raven was hanging in the balance, and I wasn't going to jeopardize that for anyone.

"So I shouldn't give a shit if you die, right?" Her eyes teared up. "You think I could survive now that I've found you?" she croaked.

I bit back a retort and didn't say another word. She wouldn't understand how much the thought of her dying was tearing me up inside. Even my inner bear was bellowing protectively.

"Fine," she said brusquely. "I'm going to make a fire. You three figure it out, but I am a part of this plan, so you'd better get your big head out of your ass and deal with it." She grabbed the packs of blankets and supplies, and then she stalked off toward the cave, muttering about stubborn, ignorant men and cavemen shifters the whole way.

Cutter and Grant waited for me to explode, but instead, I breathed in and out deeply through my nose. I needed to know what the plan was before I could make the decision on whether I could stomach putting my mate in harm's way.

"Walk me through it, Grant."

"With or without Raven?"

I snarled, and Cutter laughed until I shot him a dirty look.

# CHAPTER 53

## RAVEN

I HAD BUILT a fire in the ventilated cave and made myself a nest of blankets. The day had once again taken its toll on me, and I was ready to sleep. Making love with Bear had been an experience, one I wanted to repeat for a lifetime. First, though, we'd have to get rid of Price and his pack.

I had to stop this damn war before it started.

Since our argument outside, I hadn't spoken a single word to Bear. I wasn't going to either, not until he realized the truth.

He needed me to be the bait, plain and simple.

There was no way around it. Cutter and Grant had tried to talk to him about it, but he'd only clammed up. He refused to acknowledge that fact or that the time for action was quickly approaching and we needed a way out of this clusterfuck situation.

I poked the logs around with a stick and focused on the fire. It drew me in, and I felt like I was back in Bear's arms where I was safe, well loved, and protected from everything else happening around us. I wanted nothing more than to drag him back inside this cave and feel that all over again. Maybe then he'd realize I needed him just as much as he needed me.

The last damn thing I wanted was to lose him. After this

adventure and the life-altering discoveries, my day-to-day existence was going to be very different. Dealing with the future would be so much easier with him in the picture.

*If he weren't around—*

A shudder ran through my body from just the thought of my life without Bear. My heart ached from just thinking of never seeing him again. My hand stilled, and I tried to catch my breath. Pain like I'd never known suddenly overwhelmed me, and I felt the urge to go find him, to tell him how much he meant to me, about how I looked forward to spending the rest of my life with him.

Bear was my mate, and whatever life brought to us, we would face it together.

They were at the other end of the cave, working out the rest of their plan for tomorrow. I got to my feet and grabbed the stick they'd turned into a torch. I froze when I heard a growl behind me.

"Real cute, Cutter!" I yelled. "I'm not in the mood for games unless you're here to tell me Bear is ready to listen to his mate."

The growl grew louder and then multiplied, and then the sound echoed around the cave.

Fear gripped me and my stomach clenched. Slowly, I drew the knife I'd kept tucked in my jeans as I raised the torch higher. "Cutter? Grant?"

But a bear didn't emerge from the shadows.

"Shit."

I staggered backward as Price in his human form stepped forward, closely followed by five wolves. Someone was missing, I realized, but that was all I noticed before Price cackled darkly and reached a hand out toward me.

"Raven, sweet Raven, why don't you make this easy for us and just come here?" He leered.

"Why would I do that?" I snapped, raising the knife.

"If you want to save the life of your mate," he growled, "you will do exactly as I say."

*Hard pass on that, motherfucker.*

I lowered my arm and charged forward, aiming for Price's chest. I didn't even make it close.

Boyle snarled and lunged for me, slamming me onto the cave floor with a loud thud. The torch rolled across the floor. There was a snap, and I groaned as white-hot pain exploded up my side.

*Shit. I broke a rib, dammit. Maybe two.*

The knife was snatched from my hand. It hurt too much for me to even try to scream out in pain. Boyle kept his heavy paws on my shoulders, pinning me down, as Price leaned over me, holding the knife to my throat.

"I could kill you with one quick swipe of this blade," he whispered.

I felt the cold metal against my skin and fought the urge to flinch.

"But, sadly, I won't, or I would piss off some very important people."

He stepped back and yanked me to my feet, keeping one arm wrapped around my front and the blade at my neck.

I struggled, but the blade cut into my skin, drawing blood. It was enough to make me stop moving. "Shit."

"Now then, let's go find your mate."

My eyes narrowed. "My what?"

"Don't play coy with me, bitch. We know exactly what you are to him. Now get moving." Price shoved me forward. "We have business to deal with tonight, and then you and I are going to take a nice, long trip."

# CHAPTER 54

## BEAR

I STARED out over the drop-off and wondered if I should maybe give in first and go talk to Raven. She was stubborn, just like me, but I knew one of us would have to eventually let it go.

She was spot on. The plan to draw Price out by using her would be the right approach, but it still didn't mean I wanted her to be the bait.

Price was dangerous, and Boyle was worse. If either of them got their hands on her, I'd never forgive myself.

I swore to be her protector.

I was her mate, and it was my duty to be there for her at all times. The thought of willingly throwing her in the line of fire was making me sick.

"If you keep worrying about it, you're only going to distract yourself more," Grant warned me.

My heart thudded. "I can't help it. This is all a bit new to me, and I'm slightly overwhelmed here."

I hadn't even marked her yet, but the connection was still strong. I'd always scoffed at how much my father had doted on my mother. He'd been the strongest and gruffest man I knew, but around my mother, he'd been butter in her hands and worshipped the ground she walked on. They'd been the

happiest couple I knew, and they'd weathered clan attacks, power struggles, and the devastating blow of my sister's unexpected death.

"Raven has me wrapped around her finger already," I mused.

Grant smiled. "Yeah, I know the feeling. You'll remember it forever, and then you'll look back on these days and laugh at how ridiculous you both were."

"That bad, huh?"

"Oh yeah. This fight is just the beginning. Mate's butt heads on everything."

I rolled my eyes toward the heavens. "Shit, I'm so fucked."

Grant patted me on the shoulder with a knowing smile. "But she's damn worth it."

I grinned. "Hell yes, she is."

We joined Cutter at the other end of the plateau as he worked out the best way to lure Price's pack all up through the cave. He smiled at us, and then he sniffed the air and froze. Grant and I followed suit, and then we all turned in unison, growling and snarling.

The second I saw who it was, my heart sank to the ground and I felt a red-hot rage flooding my body. My inner bear roared and snarled.

*This isn't possible.*

*How did I let this happen?*

There had been no signs of the wolves being this close. We hadn't smelled anything, yet here they were, Price and his pack with Raven in the middle.

There was a grimace on her face, and she was favoring one side of her body. Blood reflected in the torchlight carried by a naked Boyle, wearing only a look of sadistic joy. He reached over and pushed Raven's side. She tried to keep the pain from showing on her face, but she cried out, and I roared fiercely. Cutter and Grant grabbed ahold of my shoulders, pulling me back.

"Let her go, you bastard!" I hissed.

"Oh, Bear's a wee bit touchy," Price mocked. He smiled at Boyle. "Now why would that be, Boyle?"

"I think we might have found Bear's weak spot," Boyle replied with a smirk. "What do you think?"

Price ran his hand through Raven's hair. She narrowed her gaze and tried to get away from his touch, but the blade reappeared at her neck. She froze.

"I think this beautiful Protector here is his mate. Now, isn't that interesting?" Price said.

I locked eyes with Raven, trying to tell her I was sorry. Price had gotten the jump on me, but he wasn't going to win. Somehow, I'd get Raven and me through this alive. Her lips twitched in a hopeful smile until Boyle saw it, and he grabbed her side.

"Ouch. Fuck!" she screamed.

"Leave her the hell alone," I snarled. "What the fuck do you want?"

"I want your mate," Price replied casually, as if we were discussing the weather. "There's someone who desperately wants to meet her. He'll kill her, of course, but maybe I won't let him do it right away."

I flashed my teeth and took a step forward, but Price pressed the blade harder against her throat.

"What do you think, Boyle? Looks like she could satisfy a wolf's lust for a night or two."

"I'd say a week at least. I can see her pretty long legs wrapped around me already." Boyle groaned as he sniffed Raven's neck, and then he reached up and licked the side of her face. "Moaning my name over and over again. I think she'd be good for quite a few of us actually."

Price smiled. "Then perhaps I'll have her warm my bed for a month, and then you can use her any way you want."

"Enough!" I broke free from Grant and Cutter. "Let her go, and I'll let you run home with your tails between your legs."

Price growled but didn't release her. "Now why would I do that? I have the leverage here, Bear, not you." He forced Raven

forward a few steps, keeping the blade against her skin. "I could spill her blood so easily, kill her right before your eyes. Her body would be buried in the new-fallen snow along with yours and the rest of your bastard kind."

I nodded once and lowered my head, fighting my inner bear that was pressing against my skin. Soon, I wouldn't be able to control my rage or him. "I challenge you," I growled. The words were almost inaudible.

Price's face turned pale.

"Right now. Do you dare deny me my right to a challenge? Are you that much of a fucking coward?"

Boyle cursed, and the wolves circled uneasily around us. Even Cutter and Grant looked a bit apprehensive.

Price's hand started to tremble. "You wouldn't," he finally whispered.

"I challenge you for control of your pack," I hissed.

"That is unprecedented. You can't do that."

My jaw tightened. "I just did. If I win, I will take control of your pack and weed out all those who've followed you. I will make their lives a living hell."

"And start a war in the process," Boyle stated.

"No," I argued with a mocking grin. "Any death by a challenge cannot, nor will it ever, start a war. That is shifter law. Guess you won't get everything you came for after all, Price."

# CHAPTER 55

## RAVEN

THERE WAS no way Price would agree. In bear form, Bear was easily four times Price's size. He could sit on Price and the wolf could be killed or at least severely injured.

*What the hell is Bear doing?*

"Fine," Price answered, "but I have a condition."

"Name it," Bear barked.

"We fight as humans!" Price shouted. "One on one. The winner decides the fate of the rest."

"Done," Bear replied. Then he turned to consult with Cutter and Grant.

"Boyle, I expect you to do what you must," Price whispered harshly as he shoved me into Boyle's arms, knife and all. "Do you understand my meaning?"

"Of course." Boyle bowed his head. "Kill him and let's get this over with."

I wanted to yell out a warning to Bear, but the knife was already back at my throat while Boyle held me pressed against his naked skin.

He sniffed my neck once more and sighed. "Such sweet meat. Soon, my dear, I'll get to taste you."

A shudder ran down my spine as I watched the remaining

wolves, along with Cutter and Grant, now bears, form a circle around Bear and Price. I focused on Bear's face, but he didn't look my way.

He had eyes for only one thing—Price.

It was as if his bear had taken over—if not in bear form, at least in his mind. I had no doubt Bear was going to kill Price, but I was also sure it wasn't going to be a fair fight.

Price and Bear started to step toward each other, and then they stopped and waited. I was about to ask what was going on when Price howled and lunged forward.

Price nailed Bear in the face with a one-two hit before Bear punched him in the kidney and then kicked him in the knee, knocking Price to the ground. Bear raised his foot to stomp on Price's face, but he rolled away.

Price stayed low and went for Bear's middle, trying to tackle him. I watched intently, trying to keep my gaze trained on Bear, but instead, my eyes kept going to the other wolves. They were slowly closing in tighter and moving toward Grant and Cutter. It was as if they weren't about to wait for their alpha to give the order before they attacked.

Bear grunted in pain, and I looked back to see Price kneeing him in the face. Bear staggered backward, and I yelled for him until Boyle snarled and pressed the blade against my neck, point first.

"Make another sound and you're dead," he snapped.

I glared but didn't try to say anything else.

The fight continued, but then something happened I hadn't expected.

Price half shifted, his mouth growing into that of a wolf, and he clamped down on Bear's shoulder. Bear yelled in pain as Price's teeth hit bone, and he tried to shake Bear. Now that Price was breaking the code of the challenge, Bear wasn't going to let him do it alone.

With a roar that made my bones shake, Bear shifted fully into a bear, and shreds of clothes scattered to the ground. The

shift made Price release him, and before he had a chance to react, Bear whirled around and clamped his mouth on the wolf's throat. Bear flung Price around and let him fall to the snow. Price shifted back to human form and held his bleeding throat. He staggered toward Boyle, holding out his hand for aid.

"What are you waiting for?" Price gasped. "Kill him before he kills me."

But as Bear closed in on Price, Boyle didn't move a muscle. He watched as Bear went in for the kill. Price tried to shift again, but it was too late. Bear bit down on his throat, and I watched as he yanked it out. Blood covered his face as Price's lifeless body twitched and then fell to the snow.

Price was dead. He was finally gone.

The other wolves stared in shock, but it was Boyle, the one who'd refused to save his alpha, who charged in. He shifted as he lunged for Bear and went for his back. He dug all four paws in and held on as Bear spun around, trying to dislodge him. At the same time, the other four wolves rushed toward Cutter and Grant.

It was instant chaos, and I could only stand and watch, still in shock at the sudden turn the fight had taken.

Bear was still trying to deal with Boyle, but the black wolf kept biting his shoulder and back, anything he could get ahold of. I couldn't stand it any longer, and I glanced around for a weapon. I picked up the fallen knife Boyle had dropped.

Running toward Boyle, I shoved the knife into his throat as I yelled, "Karma's a bitch!"

Boyle howled in pain as his body fell to the ground near the edge of the plateau. His claws dug into the snow and rock, trying to keep himself from going all the way over.

Tears streamed down my cheeks as my fingers fumbled over Bear's body. "Baby, please... Oh God, this is bad."

Bear wasn't moving.

I glanced up, looking for Cutter's and Grant's help, when I saw Boyle had pulled himself up and was heading straight for me.

"Oh, fuck no," I gritted out.

Bear's eyes snapped open, and he leaped up with his mouth opened wide, grabbing Boyle midair and shaking him around like a rag doll.

Boyle tried to break away, but he couldn't get loose. Bear threw him to the ground. Before he could find his feet, Bear lifted his front paws, and with all his weight, he came down on Boyle's body, crushing him.

I stared at the mangled body of the wolf. Around me, the fighting continued as Bear rushed to aid Grant and Cutter. They made quick work of the remaining wolves.

Whimpers filled the air before the eerie silence came. The wolves were all dead. Glancing around, for a minute, I thought I'd fallen into a war zone. The snow was bright red with blood, and the three bears that remained standing were covered in wounds.

One by one, they shifted back, and Bear was instantly at my side, trying to get me to my feet.

"Raven, are you all right?" he asked.

"They're all dead," I whispered. Then I winced when the pain in my side came racing back.

"It's safe. No war, and you're still here," Bear grunted.

I nodded, staring at his body. He had so many bite marks and scratches that I couldn't even tell how much blood was his. Cutter and Grant didn't look much better. We all stared at each other and then down at the butchered bodies scattered on the ground.

Cutter started chuckling and said, "Damn, I've always liked a good fight." His lips twitched, and then he broke into full-out laughter.

Grant cracked a smile next, and then Bear and I both lost it. We stood on the hill, laughing in the face of death and partially in disbelief that it was all over.

# CHAPTER 56

## RAVEN

**WEEKS Later**

With one spinning heel kick, my booted foot landed squarely in the center of Grant's chest.

"Shit," he hissed as his tightly muscled arms flapped around like a bird before his ass slammed onto the snow-covered grass.

Standing over him, I taunted, "Boom. Big trees fall hard."

"That was a lucky shot," he grouched, waving away my offered hand before jumping nimbly to his feet. Rubbing his chest, he winced.

Snickering, I pinched his cheek. He swatted me away.

"Come on. Don't be such a sore loser. Just be proud of how well you taught me to kick your ass," I crowed.

Backing away from him, I raced over to Kyle and Kristine, slapping them high fives while singing, "Another bear bites the dust."

Grant and I had been sparring for hours, and I was extra pumped from my cheering squad—Kyle and Kristine, Bear's cousin and aunt.

"What the hell are you celebrating for?" Grant grumbled, standing with his arms akimbo. "My grandmother hits harder, and she's a hundred and five." He beckoned me forward with one

finger. "Come on, baby girl. One more round. You know I like it rough."

I rolled my eyes. "You need serious help, Kinky Bear." I grabbed my bottle of water from the snow. "I'm taking a break. It'll give you enough time to pick up your shattered pride." I guzzled the water, eyeing him.

"Whatever." He walked up to me, playfully pulling my ponytail. "I can't wait for Bear to get back. You have way too much pent-up sexual aggression. He'll fuck it right out of you."

I scrunched up my nose. "Asshole."

He quickly kissed my cheek. "Love you, too, baby girl."

"Love you, too," I mumbled, trying not to get all teary-eyed from the affectionate nickname.

Grant and I had grown close over these last few weeks. He'd become the annoying big brother I never had, and I was the bratty little sister he loved and protected fiercely.

*Family. Damn, I'm one lucky chick.*

"I'm sorry. I was a little rough." I cleared my throat. "I've been a little out of sorts lately," I acknowledged.

He arched a brow. "A little?" He snorted.

I sighed. "Okay, a lot."

I was restless, agitated, and darn right horny since Bear had been called away to an emergency shifter council meeting to discuss Price and his pack's misdeeds. Cutter had gone with him, and Grant stayed behind to ensure my protection.

Even though Bear called me nightly, the hot phone sex hadn't quelled my consuming need to be taken by him in every wicked position possible.

Kristine swayed over to me, wrapping an arm around me. "Grant, cut her some slack. She's just stressed that Bear hasn't marked her yet." She clucked her tongue.

"And Bear... poor thing must be grumpy as hell. His inner bear is probably raising cane over not claiming you yet. Our beasts are primal. If they're not happy, it wreaks havoc on our human side. You're experiencing the effects."

She eyed me like a specimen under a microscope. "I've just never heard of this happening to a human, though. Anyway, it will disappear when Bear claims you. And talking of claiming, I've got to go into town to meet with the florist and caterer." She smiled at me. "You want to come with me?"

"Uh, no." My eyes nervously darted away and then came back to her. "I'm sweaty. I'd have to take a shower, get dressed, put on makeup. You know, it would take me forever." I hoped it was enough to dissuade her from pushing the issue.

I loved her, but she was driving me crazy with her elaborate planning for my and Bear's claiming ceremony—the equivalent to a celebrity wedding. What had started out as a intimate event was turning into a big extravaganza, with invitations being sent out to the who's who of the bear-shifter world.

She pinched my cheek. "All right, but I'm not letting you out of your ceremony dress fitting next week. It took too much wrangling just to get an appointment with the designer." She pulled me in for a big hug.

I tightly hugged her before pulling back. "Will you at least let me pay for the plane tickets to New York?"

The couture designer was based in Manhattan, and Kristine was arranging a luxurious girls' weekend.

"Absolutely not. You're like my daughter, and I'm paying for everything associated with the celebration."

I sighed. "It's like you don't give a shit about going broke from spending all this money on this bash. Let me help or scale the hell back on the extravagance."

"Hell no. I always go big, like Texas. Organizing this affair has been the most fun I've had in years. I need this. I want glitter and over-the-top fabulousness." Cunningly, her eyes went all puppy-dog sad. "Besides, I don't know how long I'll be around. I'm pretty old, you know."

I rolled my eyes. Kristine looked no more than fifty years old, and she ran at least thirty miles a day.

"Oh, for fuck's sake. Now you're guilt-tripping me?"

She batted her eyelashes. "Is it working?"

I scowled. "Yes. Fine. Spend your nest egg."

She laughed. "Honey, I'm a millionairess. I can make it rain money all day." She kissed my cheek. "I'm off now. Why don't you spar with Kyle a little? I think Grant's about to cry from your beatdown," she quipped. After flouncing toward her huge SUV, she drove away.

I jammed my hands on my hips, eyeing Kyle. "You want to spar?"

Kyle backed away. "No, thanks. I'm young and fragile."

Grant snorted. "Chicken shit."

Kyle rubbed his forehead, as if warding away a headache. "Call it what you want, but she's on a hormonal rampage."

I rolled my eyes before walking over to the steps to sit down. Leaning back on my elbows, I stared at the blue sky that reminded me of Bear's eyes.

Grant walked over and plopped down beside me. "What are you thinking about so hard? Work or Bear?"

I blinked. "Work? Hell no! Of course not."

After the battle with Price and his pack, I'd called the agency, telling my manager Price and his group couldn't make it in the wild and had decided to cut the trip short before taking their private jet back home. The agency had taken the news in stride. After all, they hadn't been the first group of rich clients to realize they'd bitten off more than they could chew in their quest for a romp in the great wilderness.

But when I'd told the agency about my decision to resign and finish the trek into the wilderness by myself, he'd quickly offered to triple my salary. I'd firmly declined. I'd just wanted that part of my life to be over.

I hadn't even told Halle what had really happened. Shit, she wouldn't have believed me if I'd told her the truth—that I'd found the man of my dreams and he was a bear-shifter. So I'd kept it simple and told her I needed a long sabbatical to figure out what I wanted to do next with my life.

Breaking out of my thoughts, my heart raced when I saw a familiar SUV racing up the winding road toward the cabin.

*Bear.*

When he pulled up, I barely gave him time to get out of the car before running full speed at him and jumping into his arms. He tightly clutched me against his body.

"It's my badass Bear." I kissed him hard on the lips before breaking away.

He arched down, rubbing his nose against my neck. "Damn, I missed you."

His head snapped up, and his mouth slanted over mine, ruthlessly claiming me. I trembled and gasped, loving the taste of him. He nipped my bottom lip before pulling back.

Grant and Kyle said in unison, "We're out."

I didn't care. I was like a dog with a bone, and I wanted Bear all to myself.

*But first things first.* "So how did it go?" I asked worriedly, sliding to my feet.

One arm still clutched me as the fingers of his free hand caressed my throat and jaw. "Contentious, but everyone finally agreed Price and his pack were at fault. We voted on a laundry list of sanctions against them. The remaining members of his pack don't want to start a war. They decided to take care of their problem elder, Tadeo, who ordered Price to bring you to him."

I sighed with relief. The last thing I wanted to see was a senseless bloody war between the wolf and bear-shifters.

Bear's eye twitched, a sign I now recognized as his tic that had been brought on by stress.

"Bear? What's wrong? Is it Taggert?"

"No. I debriefed him about Price and his pack, but I still have some business at the base." His jaw tightened. "Logan's still missing."

"Damn." My pulse raced.

Bear had told me about Logan, his newest enforcer and

member of his clan who'd gone missing during a surveillance mission on Price's territory.

"What are you going to do?"

"I don't know. I'm still working on a plan." He exhaled. "But problems don't stop there. I just got an urgent call from Ryker Alfero."

"Alfero?"

"He's a friend and the alpha of the toughest wolf-shifter pack in Manhattan. He says there's trouble brewing with this group called the Shadows, and it might be heading this way."

"Is there ever a moment of peace with you shifters?" I asked.

"Only when I'm with you."

He cupped my cheek, and my knees wobbled.

"At this moment, it's all about us."

"Good." I leaned up on my toes and bit his neck.

"Raven," he groaned. "I promised to take you out for dinner when I got back."

But he wasn't stopping me from licking.

"I'm hungry... for you."

"Raven," he hissed.

"Bear," I whispered. "I've been making wicked plans for my alpha. First, I'll lick you in every indecent way possible. Then I'll allow you to take me in every room in our damn cabin. I'm talking all weekend long, uninterrupted, hard-core fucking." I pulled back from his neck and bit down on his bottom lip.

*Damn, I can't get enough of his taste.*

He stretched up, tangling his hands in my hair at the back of my head. "I'm so down with that," he grunted.

I sucked on his bottom lip.

He pulled back. "But remember the small clan dinner my aunt is planning? It's this weekend."

I laid my head on his shoulder. "Small and intimate is not in Kristine's vocabulary." I raised my head and stared at him. "And she's been driving me crazy with this claiming ceremony, which is turning out to be the equivalent of a celebrity-studded wedding."

He kissed my nose and then my cheeks, and he smiled. "You'll be fine. You've met most of the clan, and they love you. The rest will, too. I promise."

"They might not." I chewed on my bottom lip. "I'm still a Protector."

He scowled. "That doesn't matter, especially now that they've heard you had a hand in killing Boyle."

I took a deep breath, not verbalizing that it didn't negate the fact that I still bore the Protector mark on my arm. "You do know after this whole claiming ceremony, you're going to be stuck with me."

"I think it's the other way around. You'll be stuck with me. I've been told I can be an asshole on occasion." He grabbed my hand, kissing the back. "Raven, I don't want to spend my life without you. You complete me. And I'll destroy any man or beast to keep you by my side."

A tear slid down my cheek. "Ditto," I whispered.

He licked my lips, and immediately, I opened up for him. He lightly brushed his tongue against mine. I moaned, the erotic sensation conjuring images in my mind of me flicking my tongue along the thick head of his throbbing manhood.

He pulled back and grunted. "It's time to claim my woman."

I twined my arms around his neck, and he effortlessly picked me up. I wrapped my legs around his waist while being carried to our large cabin. Once inside, he kicked the door closed and stomped through the cabin and into our bedroom.

With his firm hand on my back, he lowered us onto the bed, his heavy body lying over mine. With his elbows next to my head, he watched me with sexy hooded eyes. My gorgeous Bear was contemplative. His head lowered to mine, staring, predatory, and focused. My womanly center pulsed and tingled with pleasure.

I was ready for him to mark me, officially making me his for the world to see.

He lifted my leg, curling it around his waist, and he pressed

his body close, making sure I felt the hard ridge of his erection through my jeans.

Rocking his hardness against the warmth between my legs, he groaned. He took my mouth with a measured sensuality, seducing my lips and tongue.

"I missed your taste." He unhurriedly kissed me, his tongue plunging into my mouth, as his hand slid down to my hip, gripping it.

My body trembled. His hand inched up, settling firmly underneath my breast along my ribcage.

I was going crazy from his sensual kiss, his taste, his smell. I wanted nothing more but him. His every move was languid while my body screamed to be taken fast and hard.

My arms tightened around his neck, trying to urge him to go quicker. Bear shifted, pressing his hips firmly between my quivering legs. The hardness of his loins pushed against my throbbing core. Our kiss was endless.

With every lick, stroke, and flick, I sank deeper under his spell. I climbed higher as he increased the pressure of his erection against my moist center, edging me closer to an orgasm. My hips arched against him as I cried out beneath him and came.

Pushing away from me, he stood, took off his shirt, and kicked off his boots.

*Damn, I can't get enough of his tanned, muscled, smooth chest.* Running my tongue over my bottom lip, I stared at the outline of his straining shaft encased in his jeans.

"Bear, I need you inside me now."

"So impatient." He leaned forward, nipping my bottom lip.

He unsnapped my jeans before pulling them off but left on my underwear. When he extended his hand, I clasped it, letting him pull me up. He tugged my sweater over my head before tossing it across the room.

He intently stared at me while I parted my legs. I was sitting there, clad only in my lace bra and boy-cut panties.

"Stop being such a damn tease," I whispered.

He growled as his hands on my knees glided along the tops of my inner thighs. My muscles clenched. The emptiness inside me became a dull ache. Pushing my legs open, he settled between them.

My body was throbbing, open and ready to receive him. I tilted my hips, wanting him to feel my wetness. I kissed his neck, loving the taste of his saltiness on my tongue, before biting down. He hissed as a shudder ran through him.

My hands skated down to his taut ass, and his muscles bunched under my fingers as I pressed him closer. He moaned, his brows drawing down into a harsh expression. His hardness ground against my wetness as he palmed my hip.

"Fuck this taking-it-slow shit," he growled before jerking away from me.

Fumbling with the zipper of his jeans, he took them off. His swollen masterpiece was flush against his stomach. Impatiently, I ripped off my panties and bra, throwing them onto the floor.

He settled over me. I moaned as he molded my breasts with his hands while sucking and biting one rock-hard nipple until I was writhing and grinding beneath him. He journeyed down my body, pausing now and then to nip and suck at small sensitive sections of skin.

He took a minute to look at me lying there, trembling and wet, ready for him to take and possess. I gasped as he cocked my hips, kissing my moist, warm folds. His thick tongue swirled around my secret center, repeatedly flicking it, before sinking inside my throbbing core. My ass flew up, and he held me still, unrelentingly demolishing me with his wicked, clever tongue.

His soft rumbles vibrated against my clit, heightening the pleasure, almost sending me over the edge.

"Bear. Baby. Please. Stop."

His tongue continued to pillage my tight depths until I threaded my fingers through his hair and tugged hard. He snarled in the back of his throat.

"Please."

He froze, peering up at my face, before kneeling between my legs, gripping my hips, and positioning his erection at my moist, warm folds. "Please what?"

"Please, fuck me."

As if my plea splintered his self-control, his fingers wrapped around his shaft poised at my entrance. He was breathing hard as he looked into my eyes while gently pushing against me, giving me time to get used to his wide girth.

He leaned down and breathed against my lips, "You are mine." His nostrils flared as he slowly worked his way into me.

Wrapping my legs around his waist, I drove my hips up to meet him as he slammed into me. My muscles clamped around his massive fullness, and then he took me.

I let go and completely surrendered to Bear. This man was mine, and I was totally his.

Pressing his forehead against mine, he moved hard and fast. Squeezing my thighs tight around his hips, I clung to him for dear life, riding the wave of lust coiling through me. He brought his hands up to my breasts, gently cupping them, his thumbs sliding over the aching peaks. He pulled me wider, lifting my legs so my ankles were resting on his shoulders as he thrust deeper. My fingers gripped his ass, my nails digging deep.

"All of you. Mine." He nibbled his way down my throat before settling in the juncture of my neck and shoulder. He scraped his teeth over the spot, signaling to me what was to come. When he sensed my climax was near, he bit down, breaking the skin.

Instantly, I shattered, groaning and shuddering. He sucked strongly on the patch of skin he'd bitten, as if determined to leave a distinct mark that couldn't be considered as anything other than what it was.

A claiming.

As quick as that, a powerful force swept through my body before I sensed him through the clan link—not his thoughts, but his loving and confident presence.

It was done. I was his to protect as his mate and part of his clan.

Bear growled his approval as he pulled back. He admired his work and then swiped his tongue over the mark. My back arched with the explosion of pure bliss that ripped through me.

"Bear!" His name escaped my mouth in a scream so loud it hurt my ears.

"Raven," he groaned my name as his own release hit while his hardness pulsed deep inside me.

Panting and quivering with aftershocks, we stayed glued to each other, him draped over me, his face buried in the crook of my neck.

Moving ever so slightly, he whispered into my ear, "I love you, baby."

His words had my eyes snapping open. Curling all my limbs around him, I whispered into his ear, "And I love you, Bear."

The shudder that ran through him told me just how much my words affected him.

"Mate." He pulled back to look at my face as a wicked smile took over his face.

"Mine." I smiled.

I'd finally found what I'd been looking for all my life—family, love, home, and my very own big, bad sexy Bear.

THANK YOU FOR READING **BEAR'S MISSION!**

More Shifter Alpha goodness continues with **CLAIMED BY HER BEAR**!

5 scorching hot shifter romance books in one volume!

**GET A FREE SEDONA VENEZ BOOK!**

https://sedonavenez.com/free-book

# WANT FREE SEDONA VENEZ BOOKS?

Sign up for Sedona Venez's Newsletter and receive FREE BOOKS. In addition to the free stories, you will also get special pricing, exclusive previews and news of new releases.

**GET A FREE SEDONA VENEZ BOOK!**

Join Sedona's mailing list to be the first to know of new releases, free books, special prices and other author giveaways.

https://sedonavenez.com/free-book

# OTHER TITLES BY SEDONA VENEZ

**SciFi Romance**
Galaxy Alien Warriors - The Box Set
Beauty and the Alien Beast

**Paranormal Romance**
**Shifter Alphas Furever Series**
Claimed by Her Two Alphas
Claimed by Her Wolf
Claimed by Her Bear
Claimed by Her Dragon

**Paranormal Romance**
**Credence Curse Series**
When Lightning Strikes
Taming the Beast
Reason to Love

**Wolf Shifter Romance**
**Wolf Elite Series**
Operation Wolf: Gunner
Operation Wolf: Eli

Operation Wolf: Hunter

**Bears Shifter Romance**
**Bear Elite Series**
Bear's Mission

**Enemies-to-Lovers Romance**
**Dirty Secrets Series**
Twisted Lies
Twisted Lies 2
Twisted Lies 3
Twisted Lies 4

**Friends-to-Lovers Romance**
Heart of Fire

**MFM Ménage Romance**
**Standalone**
Shameless Desires

**Billionaire Boss Romance**
**Standalone**
Mr. Billionaire CEO

**Urban Fantasy Romance**
Magic Fire Collection

# WANT FREE SEDONA VENEZ BOOKS?

Sign up for Sedona Venez's Newsletter and receive FREE BOOKS. In addition to the free stories, you will also get special pricing, exclusive previews and news of new releases.

**GET A FREE SEDONA VENEZ BOOK!**

Join Sedona's mailing list to be the first to know of new releases, free books, special prices and other author giveaways.

https://sedonavenez.com/free-book